Randall Garrett

Anything You Can Do...
(Unabridged)

OK Publishing 2021

Randall Garrett
Anything You Can Do...

(Unabridged)

Published by
MUSAICUM
Books

- Advanced Digital Solutions & High-Quality book Formatting -

musaicumbooks@okpublishing.info

2021 OK Publishing

ISBN 978-80-272-7973-9

Contents

1

Like some great silver-pink fish, the ship sang on through the eternal night. There was no impression of swimming; the fish shape had neither fins nor a tail. It was as though it were hovering in wait for a member of some smaller species to swoop suddenly down from nowhere, so that it, in turn, could pounce and kill.

But still it moved and sang.

Only a being who was thoroughly familiar with the type could have told that this particular fish was dying.

In shape, the ship was rather like a narrow flounder—long, tapered, and oval in cross-section—but it showed none of the exterior markings one might expect of either a living thing or a spaceship. With one exception, the smooth silver-pink exterior was featureless.

That one exception was a long, purplish-black, roughened discoloration that ran along one side for almost half of the ship's seventeen meters of length. It was the only external sign that the ship was dying.

Inside the ship, the Nipe neither knew nor cared about the discoloration. Had he thought about it, he would have deduced the presence of the burn, but it was by far the least of his worries.

The ship sang, and the song was a song of death.

The internal damage that had been done to the ship was far more serious than the burn on the surface of the hull. It was that internal damage which occupied the thoughts of the Nipe, for it could, quite possibly, kill him.

He had, of course, no intention of dying. Not out here. Not so far, so very far, from his own people. Not out here, where his death would be so very improper.

He looked at the ball of the yellow-white sun ahead and wondered that such a relatively stable, inactive star could have produced such a tremendously energetic plasmoid, one that could still do such damage so far out. It had been a freak, of course. Such suns as this did not normally produce such energetic swirls of magnetohydrodynamic force.

But the thing had been there, nonetheless, and the ship had hit it at high velocity. Fortunately the ship had only touched the edge of the swirling cloud-otherwise the ship would have vanished in a puff of incandescence. But it had done enough. The power plants that drove the ship at ultralight velocities through the depths of interstellar space had been so badly damaged that they could only be used in short bursts, and each burst brought them closer to the fusion point. Even when they were not being used they sang away their energies in ululations of wavering vibration that would have been nerve-racking to a human being.

The Nipe had heard the singing of the engines, recognized it for what it was, realized that he could do nothing about it, and dismissed it from his mind.

Most of the instruments were powerless; the Nipe was not even sure he could land the vessel. Any attempt to use the communicator to call home would have blown his ship to atoms.

The Nipe did not want to die, but, if die he must, he did not want to die foolishly.

It had taken a long time to drift in from the outer reaches of this sun's planetary system, but using the power plants any more than was absolutely necessary would have been foolhardy.

The Nipe missed the companionship his brother had given him for so long; his help would be invaluable now. But there had been no choice. There had not been enough supplies for two to survive the long inward fall toward the distant sun. The Nipe, having discovered the fact first, had, out of his mercy and compassion, killed his brother while the other was not looking. Then, having disposed of his brother with all due ceremony, he had settled down to the long, lonely wait.

Beings of another race might have cursed the accident that had disabled the ship, or regretted the necessity that one of them should die, but the Nipe did neither, for, to him, the first notion would have been foolish and the second incomprehensible.

But now, as the ship fell ever closer toward the yellow-white sun, he began to worry about his own fate. For a while, it had seemed almost certain that he would survive long enough to build a communicator, for the instruments had already told him and his brother that the system ahead was inhabited by creatures of reasoning power, if not true intelligence, and it would almost certainly be possible to get the equipment he needed from them. Now, though, it looked as if the ship would not survive a landing. He had had to steer it away from a great gas giant, which had seriously endangered the power plants.

He did not want to die in space-wasted, forever undevoured. At least, he must die on a planet, where there might be creatures with the compassion and wisdom to give his body the proper death rites. The thought of succumbing to inferior creatures was repugnant, but it was better than rotting to feed monocells or ectogenes, and far superior to wasting away in space.

Even thoughts such as these did not occupy his mind often or for very long. Far, far better than any of those thoughts were thoughts connected with the desire and planning for survival.

The outer orbits of the gas giants had been passed at last, and the Nipe fell on through the Asteroid Belt without approaching any of the larger pieces of rock-and-metal. That he and his brother had originally elected to come into this system along its orbital plane had been a mixed blessing. To have come in at a different angle would have avoided all the debris-from planetary size on down-that is thickest in a star's equatorial plane, but it would also have meant a greater chance of missing a suitable planet unless too much reliance were placed on the already weakened power generators. As it was, the Nipe had been fortunate in being able to use the gravitational field of the gas giant to swing his ship toward the precise spot where the third planet would be when the ship arrived in the third orbit. Moreover, the planet would be retreating from the Nipe's line of flight, which would make the velocity difference that much the less.

For a while the Nipe had toyed with the idea of using the mining bases that the local life-form had set up in the Asteroid Belt as bases for his own operations, but he had decided against it. Movement would be much freer and more productive on a planet than it would be in the Belt.

He would have preferred using the fourth planet for his base. Although much smaller, it had the same reddish, arid look as his own home planet, while the third planet was three quarters drowned in water. But there were two factors that weighed so heavily against that choice that they rendered it impossible. In the first place, by far the greater proportion of the local inhabitants' commerce was between the asteroids and the third planet. Second, and even more important, the fourth world was at such a point in its orbit that the energy required to land would destroy the ship beyond any doubt.

It would have to be the third world.

As the ship fell inward, the Nipe watched his pitifully inadequate instruments, doing his best to keep tabs on every one of the ships that the local life-form used to move through space. He did not want to be spotted now, and even though the odds were against these beings having any instrument highly developed enough to spot his own craft, there was always the possibility that he might be observed optically.

So he squatted there in his ship, a centipede-like thing about five feet in length and a little less than eighteen inches in diameter, with eight articulated limbs spaced in pairs along his body, each limb ending in a five-fingered manipulatory organ that could be used equally well as hand or foot. His head, which was long and snouted, displayed two pairs of violet eyes that kept a constant watch on the indicators and screens of the few instruments that were still functioning aboard the ship.

And he waited as the ship fell toward its rendezvous with the third planet.

2

Wang Kulichenko pulled the collar of his uniform coat up closer around his ears and pulled the helmet and face-mask down a bit. It was only early October, but here in the tundra country the wind had a tendency to be chill and biting in the morning, even at this time of year. Within a week or so, he'd have to start using the power pack on his horse to electrically warm his protective clothing and the horse's wrappings, but there was no necessity for that yet. He smiled a little, as he always did when he thought of his grandfather's remarks about such "new-fangled nonsense."

"Your ancestors, son of my son," he would say, "conquered the tundra and lived upon it for thousands of years without the need of such womanish things. Are there no men any more? Are there none who can face nature alone and unafraid without the aid of artifices that bring softness?"

But Wang Kulichenko noticed-though out of politeness he never pointed it out that the old man never failed to take advantage of the electric warmth of the house when the short days came and the snow blew across the country like fine white sand. And Grandfather never complained about the lights or the television or the hot water, except to grumble occasionally that they were old and out of date and that the mail-order catalog showed that much better models were available in Vladivostok.

And Wang would remind the old man, very gently, that a paper-forest ranger only made so much money, and that there would have to be more saving before such things could be bought. He did not —*ever* —remind the old man that he, Wang, was stretching a point to keep his grandfather on the payroll as an assistant.

Wang Kulichenko patted his horse's rump and urged her softly to step up her pace just a bit. He had a certain amount of territory to cover, and although he wanted to be careful in his checking he also wanted to get home early.

Around him, the neatly-planted forest of paper-trees spread knotty, alien branches, trying to catch the rays of the winter-waning sun. Whenever Wang thought of his grandfather's remarks about his ancestors, he always wondered, as a corollary, what those same ancestors would have thought about a forest growing up here, where no forest like this one had ever grown before.

They were called paper-trees because the bulk of their pulp was used to make paper-they were of no use whatever as lumber-but they weren't really trees, and the organic chemicals that were leached from them during the pulping process were of far more value than the paper pulp.

They were mutations of a smaller plant that had been found in the temperate regions of Mars and purposely changed genetically to grow in the Siberian tundra country, where the conditions were similar to, but superior to, their natural habitat. They looked as though someone had managed to crossbreed the Joshua tree with the cypress and then persuaded the result to grow grass instead of leaves. And the photosynthesis of those grasslike blades depended on an iron-bearing compound that was more closely related to hemoglobin than to chlorophyll, giving them a rusty red color instead of the normal green of Earthly plants.

In the distance, Wang heard the whining of the wind increase, and he automatically pulled his coat a little tighter, even though he noticed no increase in the wind velocity around him.

Then, as the whine became louder, he realized that it was not the wind.

He turned his head toward the sound and looked up. For a long minute he watched the sky as the sound increased in volume, but he could see nothing at first. Then he caught a glimpse of motion, a dot that was hard to distinguish against the cloud-mottled gray sky.

What was it? An air transport in trouble? There were two transpolar routes that passed within a few hundred miles of here, but no air transport he had ever seen made a noise like that. Normally they were so high up as to be both invisible and inaudible. Must be trouble of some sort.

He reached down to the saddle pack without taking his eyes from the moving speck and took out the radiophone. He held it to his ear and thumbed the call button insistently.

Grandfather! he thought with growing irritation as the seconds passed. *Wake up! Come on, old dozer, rouse yourself from your dreams!*

At the same time, he checked his wrist compass and estimated the direction of flight of the dot and its direction from him. He'd at least be able to give the airline authorities some information if the ship fell. He wished there were some way to triangulate its height, velocity, and so on, but he had no need for that kind of thing, so he hadn't the equipment.

"Yes? Yes?" came a testy, dry voice through the earphone.

Quickly Wang gave his grandfather all the information he had on the flying thing. By now the whine had become a shrill roar and the thing in the air had become a silver-pink fish shape.

"I think it's coming down very close to here," Wang concluded. "You call the authorities and let them know that one of the aircraft is in trouble. I'll see if I can be of any help here. I'll call you back later."

"As you say," the old man said hurriedly. He cut off.

Wang was beginning to realize that the thing was a spaceship, not an airship. By this time, he could see the thing more clearly. He had never actually seen a spacecraft, but he'd seen enough of them on television to know what they looked like. This one didn't look like a standard type at all, and it didn't behave like one, but it looked and behaved even less like an airship, and Wang knew enough to be aware that he did not necessarily know every type of spaceship ever built.

In shape, it resembled the old rocket-propelled jobs that had been used for the first probings into space more than a century before, rather than the fat ovoids he was used to. But there were no signs of rocket exhausts, and yet the ship was very obviously slowing, so it must have an inertia drive.

It was coming in much lower now, on a line north of him, headed almost due east. He urged the mare forward in order to try to keep up with the craft, although it was obviously traveling at several hundred miles an hour-hardly a horse's pace.

Still, it was slowing rapidly very rapidly. Maybe...

He kept the mare moving.

The strange ship skimmed along the treetops in the distance and disappeared from sight. Then there was a thunderous crash, a tearing of wood and foliage, and a grinding, plowing sound.

For a few seconds afterward, there was silence. Then there came a soft rumble, as of water beginning to boil in some huge but distant samovar. It seemed to go on and on and on.

And there was a bluish, fluctuating glow on the horizon.

Radioactivity? Wang wondered. Surely not an atomic-powered ship without safety cutoffs in this day and age. Still, there was always the possibility that the cutoffs had failed.

He pulled out his radiophone and thumbed the call button again.

This time there was no delay. "Yes?"

"How are the radiation detectors behaving there, Grandfather?"

"One moment. I shall see." There was a silence. Then: "No unusual activity, young Wang. Why?"

Wang told him. Then he asked: "Did you get hold of the air transport authorities?"

"Yes. They have no missing aircraft, but they're checking with the space fields. The way you describe it, the thing must be a spaceship of some kind."

"I think so too. I wish I had a radiation detector here, though. I'd like to know whether that thing is hot or not. It's only a couple of miles away-maybe a little more-and if that blue glow is ionization caused by radiation, it's much too close for comfort."

"I think any source that strong would register on our detectors here, young Wang," said the old man in his dry voice. "However, I agree that it might not be the pinnacle of wisdom to approach the source too closely."

"Clear your mind of worry, Grandfather," Wang said. "I accept your words of wisdom and will go no nearer. Meanwhile, you had best put in a call to Central Headquarters Fire Control. There's going to be a blaze if I'm any judge unless they get here fast with plenty of fire equipment."

"I'll see to it," said his grandfather, cutting off.

The bluish glow in the sky had quite died away by now, and the distant rumbling was fading, too. And, oddly enough, there was not much smoke in the distance. There was a small cloud of gray vapor that rose, streamer-like, from where the glow had been, but even that was dissipated fairly rapidly in the chill breeze. Quite obviously there would be no fire. After several more minutes of watching, he was sure of it. There couldn't have been much heat produced in the explosion-if it could really be called an explosion.

Then Wang saw something moving in the trees between himself and the spot where the ship had come down. He couldn't see quite what it was, there in the dimness under the hanging, grasslike red strands from the trees, but it looked like someone crawling.

"Halloo, there!" he called out. "Are you hurt?"

There was no answer. Perhaps whoever it was did not understand Russian. Wang's command of English wasn't too good, but he called out in that language.

Still there was no answer. Whoever it was had crawled out of sight.

Then he realized it couldn't be anyone crawling. No one could even have run the distance between himself and the ship in the time since it had hit, much less crawled.

He frowned. A wolf, then? Possibly. They weren't too common, but there were still some of them around.

He unholstered the heavy pistol at his side.

And as he slid the barrel free, he became the first human being ever to see the Nipe.

For an instant, as the Nipe came out from behind a tree fifteen feet away, Wang Kulichenko froze as he saw those four baleful violet eyes glaring at him from the snouted head. Then he jerked up his pistol to fire.

He was much too late. His reflexes were too slow by far. The Nipe launched himself across the intervening space in a blur of speed that would have made a leopard seem slow. Two of the alien's hands slapped aside the weapon with a violence that broke the man's wrist, while other hands slammed at the human's skull.

Wang Kulichenko hardly had time to be surprised before he died.

3

The Nipe stood quietly for a moment, looking down at the thing he had killed. His stomachs churned with disgust. He ignored the fading hoofbeats of the slave-animal from which he had knocked the thing that lay on the ground with a crushed skull. The slave-animal was unintelligent and unimportant.

This was-had been-the intelligent one.

But so slow! So incredibly slow! And so weak and soft!

It seemed impossible that such a poorly equipped beast could have survived long enough on any world to become the dominant life-form.

Then again, perhaps it was not the dominant form. Perhaps it was merely a higher form of slave-animal. He would have to do more investigating.

He picked up the weapon the thing had been carrying and examined it carefully. The mechanism was unfamiliar, but a glance at the muzzle told him it was a projectile weapon of some sort. The spiraling grooves in the barrel were obviously intended to impart a spin to the projectile, to give it gyroscopic stability while in flight.

He tossed the weapon aside. Now there was a certain compassion in his thoughts as he looked again at the dead thing. It must surely have thought it was faced with a wild animal, the Nipe decided. Surely no being would carry a weapon for use against members of its own or another intelligent species.

He examined the rest of the equipment on the thing. There was very little further information. The fabric in which it wrapped itself was crude, but ingeniously put together, and its presence indicated that the being needed some sort of protection against the temperature. It appeared to have a thermal insulating quality. Evidently the creature was used to a warmer climate. That served as additional information to help substantiate his observation from space that the areas farther south were the ones containing the major centers of population. The tilt of this planet on its axis would tend to give the weather a cyclic variation, but it appeared that the areas around the poles remained fairly cold even when the incidence of radiation from the primary was at maximum.

It would have been good, he decided, if he had stopped the slave-animal. There had been more equipment on the thing's back which would have given him more information upon which to base a judgment as to the level of civilization of the dead being. That, however, was no longer practicable, so he dismissed the thought from his mind.

The next question was, what should he do with the body?

Should he dispose of it properly, as one should with a validly slain foe?

It didn't seem that he could do anything else, and yet his stomachs wanted to rebel at the thought. After all, it wasn't as if the thing were really a proper being. It was astonishing to find another intelligent race; none had ever been found before, although the existence of such had been postulated. There were certain criteria that must be met by any such beings, however.

It must have manipulatory organs, such as this being very obviously did have-organs very much like his own. But there were only two, which argued that the being lacked dexterity. The organs for walking were encased in protective clothing too stiff to allow them to be used as manipulators.

He ripped off one of the boots and looked at the exposed foot. The thumb was not opposed. Obviously such an organ was not much good for manipulation.

He pried open the eating orifice and inspected it carefully. Ah! The creature was omnivorous, judging by its teeth. There were both rending and grinding teeth. That certainly argued for intelligence, since it showed that the being could behave in a gentlemanly fashion. Still, it was not conclusive.

If they *were* intelligent, it was most certainly necessary for him to show that he was also civilized and a gentleman. On the other hand, the slowness and lack of strength of this particular specimen argued that the species was of a lower order than the Nipe, which made the question even more puzzling.

In the end, the question was rendered unnecessary for the time being, since the problem was taken out of his hands.

A sound came from the ground a few yards away. It was an insistent buzzing. Cautiously, the Nipe approached the thing.

Buzz-buzz! Buzz-buzz-buzzzzzz!

It was an instrument of some kind. He recognized it as the device that he had seen the dead being speak into while he, himself, had been watching from the concealment of the undergrowth, trying to decide whether or not to approach. The device was obviously a communicator of some kind, and someone at the other end was trying to make contact.

If it were not answered, whoever was calling would certainly deduce that something had gone wrong at this end. And, of course, there was no way for it to be answered.

It would be necessary, then, to leave the body here for others of its kind to find. Doubtless they would dispose of it properly.

He would have to leave quickly. It was necessary that he find one of their centers of production or supply, and he would have to do it alone, with only the equipment he had on him. The utter destruction of his ship had left him seriously hampered.

He began moving, staying in the protection of the trees. He had no way of knowing whether investigators would come by air or on the slave-animals, and there was no point in taking chances.

His sense of ethics still bothered him. It was not at all civilized to leave a body at the mercy of lesser animals or monocells in that fashion. What kind of monster would they think he was?

Still, there was no help for it. If they caught him, they might think him a lower animal and shoot him. He would not have put an onus like that upon them.

He moved on.

4

Government City was something of a paradox. It was the largest capital city, in terms of population, that had ever been built on Earth, and yet, again in terms of population, it was nowhere near as large as Tokyo or London. The solution to the paradox lies in discovering that the term "population" is used in two different senses, thus exposing the logical fallacy of the undistributed middle. If, in referring to London or Tokyo, the term "population" is restricted to those and only those who are actively engaged in the various phases of actual government-as it is when referring to Government City-the apparent paradox resolves itself.

Built on the slagged-down remains of New York's Manhattan Island, which had been destroyed by a sun bomb during the Holocaust nearly a century before, Government City occupied all but the upper three miles of the island, and the population consisted almost entirely of men and women engaged, either directly or indirectly, in the business of governing a planet. There were no shopping centers and no entertainment areas. The small personal flyer, almost the same size as the old gasoline-driven automobile, could, because of its inertia drive, move with the three-dimensional ability of a hummingbird, so the rivers that cut the island off from the mainland were no barrier. The shopping and entertainment centers of Brooklyn, Queens, and Jersey were only five minutes away, even through the thickest, slowest-moving traffic. It was the personal flyer, not the clumsy airplane, that had really eliminated distance along with national boundaries.

The majority of the government officers' homes were off the island, too, but this commuting did not cause any great fluctuation of the island's population. A city that governs a planet must operate at full capacity twenty-four hours a day, and there was a "rush hour" every three hours as the staggered six-hour shifts changed.

Physically the planet still revolved about the sun; politically, Earth revolved around Government City.

In one of the towering buildings a group of men sat comfortably in a medium-sized room, watching a screen that, because of the three-dimensional quality and the color fidelity of the scene it showed, might have been a window, except that the angle was wrong. They were looking down from an apparent height of forty feet on a clearing in a paper-tree forest in Siberia.

The clearing was not a natural one. The trees had been splintered, uprooted, and pushed away from the center of the long, elliptical area. The center of the area was apparently empty.

One of the men, whose fingers were touching a control panel in the arm of his chair, said: "That is where the ship made its crash landing. As you can see from the relatively light damage, it was moving at no great speed when it hit. From the little information we have-mostly from a momentary radar recording made when the incoming vessel was picked up for a few seconds by the instruments of Transpolar Airways, when it crossed the path of one of their freight orbits-it is estimated that the craft was decelerating at between fifteen and seventeen gravities. The rate of change of acceleration in centimeters per second cubed is unknown, but obviously so small as to be negligible.

"This picture was taken by the fire prevention flyers that came in response to an urgent call by the assistant of the forest ranger who was in charge of this section."

"There was no fire?" asked one of the other men, looking closely at the image.

"None," said the speaker. "We can't yet say what actually happened to the ship. We have only a couple of hints. One of our weather observers, orbiting at four hundred miles, picked up a tremendous flash of hard ultraviolet radiation in the area around the three thousand Ångstrom band. There must have been quite a bit of shorter wavelength radiation, but the Earth's atmosphere would filter most of it out.

"A recording of the radiophone discussion between the ranger and his assistant is the only other description we have. The ranger described a bluish glow over the site. Part of that may have been due to actual blue light given off by the-well, call it 'burning'; that word will do for now. But some of the blue glow was almost certainly due to ionization of the air by the hard ultraviolet. Look at this next picture."

The scene remained the same, and yet there was a definite change.

"This was taken three days later. If you'll notice, the normal rust-red of the foliage has darkened to a purplish brown in the area around the crash site. Now a Martian paper-tree, even in the mutated form, is quite resistant to U-V, since it evolved under the thin atmosphere of Mars, which gives much less protection from ultraviolet radiation than Earth's does. Nevertheless, those trees have a bad case of sunburn."

"And no heat," said a third man. "Wow."

"Oh, there was some heat, but not anywhere near what you'd expect. The nearer trees were rather dry, as though they'd been baked, but only at the surface, and the temperature probably didn't rise much above one-fifty centigrade."

"How about X rays?" asked still another man. "Anything shorter than a hundred Ångstroms detected?"

"No. If there was any radiation that hard, there was no detector close enough to measure it. We doubt, frankly, whether there was any."

"The 'fire', if you want to call it that, must have stunk up the place pretty badly," said one of the men dryly.

"It did. There were still traces of ozone and various oxides of nitrogen in the air when the fire prevention flyers arrived. The wind carried them away from the ranger, so he didn't get a whiff of them."

"And this-this 'fire'—it destroyed the ship completely?"

"Almost completely. There are some lumps of metal around, but we can't make anything of them yet. Some of them are badly fused, but that damage was probably done before the ship landed. Certainly there was not enough heat generated after the crash to have done that damage." His hand moved over the control panel in the armrest of his chair, and the scene changed.

"This was taken from the ground. Those lumps you see are the pieces of metal I was talking about. Notice the fine white powdery ash, which caused the white spot that you could see from the air. That is evidently all that is left of the hull and the rest of the ship. None of it is radioactive.

"Random samplings from various parts of the area show that the ash consists of magnesium, lithium, and beryllium carbonates."

"You don't mean oxides?" said one of the others.

"No. I mean carbonates. And some silicate. We estimate that the remaining ash could not have constituted more than ten percent of the total mass of the hull of the ship. The rest of it vaporized, apparently into carbon dioxide and water."

"Some kind of plastic?" hazarded one of the men.

"Undoubtedly, if you want to use a catchall term like 'plastic'. But what kind of plastic goes to pieces like that?"

That rhetorical question was answered by a silence.

"There's no doubt," said one of them after a moment, "that circumstantial evidence alone would link the alien with the ship. But have you any more conclusive evidence?"

The hand moved, and the scene changed again. It was not a pretty scene.

"That, as you can see, is a closeup of the late Wang Kulichenko, the forest ranger who was the only man ever to see the alien ship before it was destroyed. Notice the peculiar bruises on the cheek and ear-the whole side of the head. The pattern is quite similar on the other side of the head."

"It looks-umm-rather like a handprint."

"It is. Kulichenko was slapped —*hard!* —on both sides of his head. It crushed his skull." There was an intake of breath.

"This next picture —" The scene changed. " —shows the whole body. If you'll look closely you'll see the same sort of prints on the ground around it. All very much like handprints. And that ties in very well with the photographs of the alien itself."

"There's no doubt about it," said one of the others. "The connection is definitely there."

The lecturer's hand moved over the control panel again, and suddenly the screen was filled with the image of an eight-limbed horror with four glaring violet eyes. In spite of themselves, a couple of the men gasped. They had seen photographs before, but a full-sized three-dimensional color projection is something else again.

"Until three weeks ago, we knew of no explanation for the peculiar happenings in northern Asia. After eight months of investigation, we found ourselves up against a blank wall. Nothing could account for that peculiar fire nor for the queer circumstances surrounding the death of the forest ranger. The investigators suspected an intelligent alien life-form, but-well, the notion simply seemed too fantastic. Attempts to trail the being by means of those peculiar 'footprints' failed. They ended at a riverbank and apparently never came out again. We know now that it swam downstream for over a hundred miles. Little wonder it got away.

"Even those investigators who suspected something non-human pictured the being as humanoid, or, rather, anthropoid in form. The prints certainly suggest those of an ape. There appeared to be four of them, judging by the prints-although frequently there were only three and sometimes only two. It all depended on how many of his 'feet' he felt like walking on."

"And then the whole herd of them dived into a river and never came up again, eh?" remarked one of the listeners.

"Exactly. You can see why the investigators kept the whole thing quiet. Nothing more was seen, heard, or reported for eight months.

"Then, three weeks ago, a non-vision phone call was received by the secretary of the Board of Regents of the Khrushchev Memorial Psychiatric Hospital in Leningrad. An odd, breathy voice, speaking very bad Russian, offered a meeting. It was the alien. He managed to explain, in spite of the language handicap, that he did not want to be mistaken for a wild animal, as had happened with the forest ranger.

"The secretary, Mr. Rogov, felt that the speaker was probably deranged, but, as he said later, there was something about that voice that didn't sound human. He said he would make arrangements, and asked the caller to contact him again the next day. The alien agreed. Rogov then —"

"Excuse me," one of the men interrupted apologetically, "but did he learn Russian all by himself, or has it been established that someone taught him the language?"

"The evidence is that he learned it all by himself, from scratch, in those eight months."

"I see. Excuse my interruption. Go on."

"Mr. Rogov was intrigued by the story he had heard. He decided to check on it. He made a few phone calls, asking questions about a mysterious crash in the paper forests, and the death of a forest ranger. Naturally those who *did* know were curious about how Mr. Rogov had learned so much about the incident. He told them.

"By the time the alien made his second call, a meeting had been arranged. When he showed up, those of the Board who were still of the opinion that the call had been made by a crank or a psychosis case changed their minds very rapidly."

"I can see why," murmured someone.

"The alien's ability to use Russian is limited," the speaker continued. "He picked up vocabulary and grammatical rules very rapidly, but he seemed completely unable to use the language beyond discussion of concrete objects and actions. His mind is evidently too alien to enable him to do more than touch the edges of human communication.

"For instance, he called himself 'Nipe' or 'Neep', but we don't know whether that refers to him as an individual or as a member of his race. Since Russian lacks both definite and indefinite articles, it is possible that he was calling himself 'a Nipe' or 'the Nipe'. Certainly that's the impression he gave.

"In the discussions that followed, several peculiarities were noticed, as you can read in detail in the reports that the Board and the Government staff prepared. For instance, in discussing mathematics the Nipe seemed to be completely at a loss. He apparently thought of mathematics as a *spoken* language rather than a *written* one and could not progress beyond simple diagrams. That's just one small example. I'm just trying to give you a brief outline now; you can read the reports for full information.

"He refused to allow any physical tests on his body, and, short of threatening him at gunpoint, there was no practicable way to force him to accede to our wishes. Naturally, threats were out of the question."

"Couldn't X rays have been taken surreptitiously?" asked one of the men.

"It was discussed and rejected. We have no way of knowing what his tolerance to radiation is, and we didn't want to harm him. The same applies to using any anesthetic gas or drug to render him unconscious. There was no way to study his metabolism without his co-operation unless we were willing to risk killing him."

"I see. Naturally we couldn't harm him."

"Exactly. The Nipe had to be treated as an emissary from his home world-wherever that may be. He has killed a man, yes. But that has to be allowed as justifiable homicide in self-defense, since the forester had drawn a gun and was ready to fire. Nobody can blame the late Wang Kulichenko for that, but nobody can blame the Nipe, either."

They all looked for a moment in silence at the violet eyes that gazed at them from the screen.

"For nearly three weeks," the speaker went on, "humans and Nipe tried to arrive at a meeting of minds, and, just when it would seem that such a meeting was within grasp, it would fade away into mist. It was only three days ago that the Russian psychologists and psychiatrists realized that the reason the Nipe had come to them was because he had thought that the Board of Regents of the hospital was the ruling body of that territory."

Someone chuckled, but there was no humor in it.

"Now we come to yesterday morning," said the speaker. "This is the important part at this very moment, because it explains why I feel we must immediately take steps to tell the public what has happened, why I feel that it is necessary to put a man like Colonel Walther Mannheim in charge of the Nipe affair and keep him in charge until the matter is cleared up. Because the public is going to be scared witless if we don't do something to reassure them."

"What happened yesterday morning, Mr. President?" one of the men asked.

"The Nipe got angry, lost his temper, went mad-whatever you want to call it. At the morning meeting he simply became more and more incomprehensible. The psychologists were trying to see if the Nipe had any religious beliefs, and, if so, what they were. One of them, a Dr. Valichek, was explaining the various religious sects and rites here on Earth. Suddenly, with no warning whatever, the Nipe chopped at Valichek's throat with an open-hand judo cut, killing him. He killed two more men before he leaped out of the window and vanished.

"No trace of him was found until late last night. He killed another man in Leningrad-we have since discovered that it was for the purpose of stealing his personal flyer. The Nipe could be anywhere on Earth by now."

"How was the man killed, Mr. President? With bare hands, as the others were?"

"We have no way of knowing. Identification of the body was made difficult by the fact that every shred of flesh had been stripped away. It had been gnawed-literally *eaten* —to the bone!"

FIRST INTERLUDE

The big man with the tiny child on his shoulder pushed through the air curtain that kept the warm humid air out of the shop.

"There," he said to the little boy softly, turning his head to look up into the round, chubby, smiling face. "There. Isn't that nicer, huh? Isn't that better than that hot old air outside?"

"Gleefle-ah," said the child with a grin.

"Oh, come on, boy. I've heard you manage bigger words than that. Or is it your brother?" He chuckled and headed toward the drug counter.

"Hey, Jim!"

The big man brought himself up short and turned-carefully, so as not to jiggle the baby on his shoulder. When he saw the shorter, thinner man, he grinned hugely. "Jinks! By God! Jinks! Watch it! Don't shake the hand too hard or I'll drop this infant. God damn, man, I thought you were in Siberia!"

"I was, Jim, but a man can't stay in Siberia forever. Is that minuscule lump of humanity your own?"

"Yup, yup. So I've been led to believe. Say hello to your Uncle Jinks, young 'un. C'mon, say hello."

The child jammed the three fingers of his left hand into his mouth and refused to say a word. His eyes widened with an unfathomable baby-emotion.

"Well, he's got your eyes," said the thinner man. "Fortunately, he's going to look like his mother instead of being ugly. He *is* a he, isn't he?"

"That's right. Mother's looks, father's plumbing. I got another just like him, but his mother's taking the other one to the doctor to get rid of the sniffles. Don't want this one to catch it."

"Twins?"

"Naw," said the big man sarcastically, "Octuplets. The Government took seventy-five percent for taxes."

"Ask a silly question, get a silly answer," the smaller man said philosophically.

"Yup. So how's the Great Northern Wasteland, Jinks?"

"Cold," said Jinks, "but it's not going to be a wasteland much longer, Jim. Those Martian trees are going to be a big business in fifteen years. There'll be forests all over the tundra. They'll make a hell of a fine income crop for those people. We've put in over five thousand square miles in seedlings during the past five years. The first ones will be ready to harvest in ten years, and from then on, it will be as regular as clockwork."

"That's great. Great. How long'll you be in town, Jinks?"

"About a week. Then I've got to head back to Siberia."

"Well, look, could you drop around some evening? We could kill off a few bottles of beer after we eat one of Ellen's dinners. How about it?"

"I'd love to. Sure Ellen won't mind?"

"She'll be tickled pink to see you. How about Wednesday?"

"Sure. I'm free Wednesday evening. But you ask Ellen first. I'll give you a call tomorrow evening to make sure I won't get a chair thrown at me when I come in the door."

"Great! I'll let her do the inviting, then."

"Look," Jinks said, "I've got half an hour or so right now. Let me buy you a beer. Or don't you want to take the baby in?"

"No, it's not that, but I've got to run. I just dropped in to get a couple of things, then I have to get on out to the plant. Some piddling little thing came up, and they want to talk to me about it." He patted the baby's leg. "Nothing personal, pal," he said in a soft aside.

"You taking the baby into an atomic synthesis plant?" Jinks asked.

"Why not? It's safe as houses. You've still got the Holocaust Jitters, my friend. He'll be safer there than at home. Besides, I can't just leave him in a locker, can I?"

"I guess not. Just don't let him get his genes irradiated," Jinks said, grinning. "So long. I'll call tomorrow at twenty hundred."

"Fine. See you then. So long."

The big man adjusted the load on his shoulder and went on toward the counter.

5

Two-fifths of a second. That was all the time Bart Stanton had from the first moment his supersensitive ears heard the first faint whisper of metal against leather.

He made good use of the time.

The noise had come from behind and slightly to the left of him, so he drew his left-hand weapon and spun to the left as he dropped to a crouch. He had turned almost completely around, drawn his gun, and fired three shots before the other man had even leveled his own weapon.

The bullets from Stanton's gun made three round spots on the man's jacket, almost touching each other, and directly over the heart. The man blinked stupidly for a moment, looking down at the spots.

"My God," he said softly.

Then he returned his own weapon slowly to its holster.

The big room was noisy. The three shots had merely added to the noise of the gunfire that rattled intermittently around the two men. And even that gunfire was only a part of the cacophony. The tortured molecules of the air in the room were so besieged by the beat of drums, the blare of trumpets, the crackle of lightning, the rumble of heavy machinery, the squawks and shrieks of horns and whistles, the rustle of autumn leaves, the machine-gun snap of popping popcorn, the clink and jingle of falling coins, and the yelps, bellows, howls, roars, snarls, grunts, bleats, moos, purrs, cackles, quacks, chirps, buzzes, and hisses of a myriad of animals, that each molecule would have thought that it was being shoved in a hundred thousand different directions at once if it had had a mind to think with.

The noise wasn't deafening, but it was certainly all-pervasive.

Bart Stanton had reholstered his own weapon and half opened his lips to speak when he heard another sound behind him.

Again he whirled, his guns in his hands-both of them this time-and his forefingers only fractions of a millimeter from the point that would fire the hair triggers.

But he did not fire.

The second man had merely shifted the weapons in his holsters and then dropped his hands away.

The noise, which had been flooding the room over the speaker system, died instantly.

Stanton shoved his guns back into place and rose from his crouch. "Real cute," he said, grinning. "I wasn't expecting that one."

The man he was facing smiled back. "Well, Bart, perhaps we have proved our point. What do you think, Colonel?" The last was addressed to the third man, who was still standing quietly, looking worried and surprised about the three spots on his jacket that had come from the special harmless projectiles in Stanton's gun.

Colonel Mannheim was four inches shorter than Stanton's five-ten, and was fifteen years older. But in spite of the differences, he would have laughed if anyone had told him five minutes before that he couldn't outdraw a man who was standing with his back turned.

His bright blue eyes, set deep beneath craggy brows in a tanned face, looked speculatively at the younger man.

"Incredible," he said gently. "Absolutely incredible." Then he looked at the other man, a lean civilian with mild blue eyes a shade lighter than his own. "All right, Farnsworth; I'm convinced. You and your staff have quite literally created a superman. Anyone who can stand in a noise-filled room and hear a man draw a gun twenty feet behind him is incredible enough. The fact that he could and did outdraw and outshoot me after I had started-well, that's almost beyond comprehension."

He looked back at Bart Stanton. "What's your opinion? Do you think you can handle the Nipe, Stanton?"

Stanton paused imperceptibly before answering, while his ultrafast mind considered the problem before arriving at a decision. Just how much confidence should he show the colonel?

Mannheim was a man with tremendous confidence in his own abilities, but who was nevertheless capable of recognizing that there were men who were his superiors in one field or another.

"If I can't dispose of the Nipe," Stanton said, "no one can."

Colonel Mannheim nodded slowly. "I believe you're right," he said at last. His voice was firm with inner conviction. He shot a glance at Farnsworth. "How about the second man?"

Farnsworth shook his head. "He'll never make it. In another two years we can put him into reasonable shape again, but his nervous system just couldn't stand the gaff."

"Can we get another man ready in time?"

"Hardly. We can't just pick a man up off the street and turn him into a superman. Even if we could find another subject with Bart's genetic possibilities, it would take more time than we have to spare."

"No way at all of cutting the time down?"

"This isn't magic, Colonel," Farnsworth said. "You don't change a nobody into a physical and mental giant by saying *abracadabra* or by teaching him how to pronounce *shazam* properly."

"I'm aware of that," said the colonel without rancor. "It's just that I keep feeling that five years of work on Mr. Stanton should have taught you enough to be able to repeat the process in less time."

Farnsworth repeated the head-shaking. "Human beings aren't machines, Colonel. They require time to heal, time to learn, time to integrate themselves. Remember that, in spite of our increased knowledge of anesthesia, antibiotics, viricides, and obstetrics, it still takes nine months to produce a baby. We're in the same position, if not more so. After all, we can't even allow for a premature delivery."

"I know," said Mannheim.

"Besides," Dr. Farnsworth continued, "Stanton's body and nervous system are now close to the theoretical limit for human tissue. I'm afraid you don't realize what kind of mental stability and organization are required to handle the equipment he has now."

"I'm sure I don't," Colonel Mannheim agreed. "I doubt if anyone besides Stanton himself *really* knows." He looked at Bart Stanton. "That's it then, son. You're it. You're the only answer we've found so far. And the only answer visible in the foreseeable future to the problem posed by the Nipe."

The colonel's face seemed to darken. "Ten years," he said in a low voice. "Ten years that inhuman monster has been loose on Earth. He's become a legend. He's replaced Satan, the Bogeyman, Frankenstein's monster, and Mumbo Jumbo, Lord of the Congo, in the public mind. Read the newsfacs, watch the newscasts. Take a look at popular fiction. He's everywhere at once. He can do anything. He's taken on the attributes of the djinn, the vampire, the ghoul, the werewolf, and every other horror and hobgoblin that the mind of man has conjured up in the past half million years."

"That's hardly surprising, Colonel," Bart Stanton said with a wry smile. "If a human being had gone on a ten-year rampage of robbery and murder, showing himself as callously indifferent to human life and property as you and I would be to the life and property of a cockroach, and if, in addition, he proved impossible to catch, such a person would be looked upon as a demon too. And if you add to that the fact that the Nipe is *not* human, that he is as frightening in appearance as he is in actions, what can you expect?"

"I agree," said Dr. Farnsworth. "Look at Jack the Ripper and consider how he terrorized London a couple of centuries ago."

"I know," said Colonel Mannheim. "There have been human criminals whose actions could be described as 'inhuman', but the Nipe has some touches that few human criminals have thought of and almost none would have the capacity to execute. If he has time to spare, his victims become an annoying problem in identification when they're found. He leaves nothing but well-gnawed bones. And by 'time to spare', I mean twenty or thirty minutes. The damned monster has a very efficient digestive tract, if nothing else. He eats like a shrew."

"And if he doesn't have time, he beats them to death," Bart Stanton said thoughtfully.

Colonel Mannheim frowned. "Not exactly. According to the evidence —"

Dr. Farnsworth interrupted him. "Colonel, let's go into the lounge, shall we? Aside from the fact that standing around in an empty chamber like this isn't the most comfortable way to discuss the fate of mankind, this room is scheduled for other work."

Colonel Mannheim grinned, caught up by the touch of lightness that the biophysicist had injected into the conversation. "Very well. I could do with some coffee, if you have some."

"All you want," said Dr. Farnsworth, leading the way toward the door of the chamber and opening it. "Or, if you'd prefer something with a little more power to it...."

"Thanks, no," said Mannheim. "Coffee will do fine. How about you, Stanton?"

Bart Stanton shook his head. "I'd love to have some coffee, but I'll leave the alcohol alone. I'd just have the luck to be finishing a drink when our friend, the Nipe, popped in on us. And when I do meet him, I'm going to need every microsecond of reflex speed I can scrape up."

They walked down a soft-floored, warmly lit corridor to an elevator which whisked them up to the main level of the Neurophysical Institute Building.

Another corridor led them to a room that might have been the common room of one of the more exclusive men's clubs. There were soft chairs and shelves of books and reading tables and smoking stands, all quietly luxurious. There was no one in the room when the three men entered.

"We can have some privacy here," Dr. Farnsworth said. "None of the rest of the staff will come in until we're through."

He walked over to a table, where an urn of coffee radiated soft warmth. "Cream and sugar over there on the tray," he said as he began to fill cups.

The cups were filled and the three men sat down in a triangle of chairs before any of them spoke again. Then Bart Stanton said:

"I made the remark that if the Nipe doesn't have time to eat his victims he just beats them to death, and you started to say something, Colonel."

Colonel Mannheim took a sip from his cup before he spoke. "Yes. I was going to say that, according to the evidence we have, he *always* beats his victims to death, whether he manages to eat them or not."

"Oh?" Stanton looked thoughtful.

"Oh, he's not cruel about it," the colonel said. "He kills quickly and neatly. The thing is that he never, under any circumstances, uses any weapons except the weapons that nature gave him-hands or feet or claws or teeth. He never uses a gun or a knife or even a club. Dr. Yoritomo has some theories about that which I won't go into now. He'll tell you about them pretty soon."

Stanton thought about the Japanese scientist and smiled. "I know. Dr. Yoritomo has threatened to tell me all kinds of theories."

"And believe me he will," said Mannheim with a soft chuckle. He took another sip of his coffee and then looked up at Stanton. "You've been through five years of hell, Mr. Stanton. In addition, you've been pretty much isolated here. Dr. Farnsworth, here, has tried to keep you informed, but, as I understand it, it has only been during the last few months that you've actually been able to absorb and retain information reliably. At least, that's the report I get. How do you feel about it?"

Bart Stanton thought for a moment. It was true that he'd been out of touch with what had been going on outside the walls of the Neurophysical Institute for the past five years. In spite of the reading he'd done and the newscasts he'd watched and the TV tapes he'd seen, he still had no real feeling for the situation.

There had been long hazy periods during that five years. He had undergone extensive glandular and neural operations of great delicacy, many of which had resulted in what could have been agonizing pain without the use of suppressors. As a result of those operations, he possessed a biological engine that, for sheer driving power and nicety of control, surpassed any other known to exist or to have ever existed on Earth-with the possible exception of the Nipe. But those five years of rebuilding and retraining had left a gap in his life.

Several of the steps required to make the conversion from man to superman had resulted in temporary insanity; the wild, swinging imbalances of glandular secretions seeking a new balance, the erratic misfirings of neurons as they attempted to adjust to higher nerve-impulse velocities, and the sheer fatigue engendered by cells that were acting too rapidly for a lagging excretory system, all had contributed to periods of greater or lesser abnormality.

That he was sane now, there was no question. But there were holes in his memory that still had to be filled.

He admitted as much to Colonel Mannheim.

"I see." The colonel rubbed one hand along the angle of his jaw, considering his next words. "Can you give me, in your own words, a general summary of the type of thing the Nipe has been doing?"

"I think so," Stanton said.

His verbal summary was succinct and accurate. The loot that the Nipe had been stealing had, at first, seemed to be a hodgepodge of everything. It was unpredictable. Money, as such, he apparently had no use for. He had taken gold, silver, and platinum, but one raid for each of these elements had evidently been enough, with the exception of silver, which had required three raids over a period of four years. Since then, he hadn't touched silver again.

He hadn't yet tried for any of the radioactives except radium. He'd taken a full ounce of that in five raids, but hadn't attempted to get his hands on uranium, thorium, plutonium, or any of the other elements normally associated with atomic energy. Nor had he tried to steal any of the fusion materials-the heavy isotopes of hydrogen or any of the lithium isotopes. Beryllium had been taken, but whether there was any significance in the thefts or not, no one knew.

There was a pattern in the thefts and robberies, nonetheless. They had begun small and had increased. Scientific and technical instruments-oscilloscopes, X-ray generators, radar equipment, maser sets, dynostatic crystals, thermolight resonators, and so on-were stolen complete or gutted for various parts. After a while, he had gone on to bigger things-whole aircraft, with their crews, had vanished.

That he had not committed anywhere near all the crimes that had been attributed to him was certain; that he *had* committed a great many of them was equally certain.

There was no doubt at all that his loot was being used to make instruments and devices of unknown kinds. He had used several of them on his raids. The one that could apparently phase out any electromagnetic frequency up to about a hundred thousand megacycles-including sixty-cycle power frequencies-was considered a particularly cute item. So was the gadget that reduced the tensile strength of concrete to about that of a good grade of marshmallow.

After he had been operating for a few years, there was no installation on Earth that could be considered Nipe-proof for more than a few minutes. He struck when and where he wanted and took whatever he needed.

It was manifestly impossible to guard against the Nipe, since no one knew what sort of loot might strike his fancy next, and there was therefore no way of knowing where or how he would hit next.

Nor could he ever be found after one of his raids. They were plotted and followed through with diabolical accuracy and thoroughness. He struck, looted, and vanished. And he wasn't seen again until his next strike.

Colonel Mannheim, who had carefully puffed a cigar alight and smoked it thoughtfully during Stanton's recitation, dropped the remains of the cigar into an ash receptacle. "Accurate but incomplete," he said quietly. "You must have made some guesses. I'd like to hear them."

Stanton finished the last of his coffee and glanced at Dr. Farnsworth. The biophysicist was thoughtfully looking down at his own cup, his expression unreadable.

All right, Stanton thought, *he's looking for something. I'll let him have both barrels and see if I hit the target.*

"I've thought about it," he admitted. He got up, went over to the coffee urn, and refilled his cup. "I've got a pet theory of my own. It's just a notion, really. I wouldn't dare reduce it to syllogistic form, because it might not hold much water, logically speaking. But the evidence seems conclusive enough to me."

He walked back to his seat. Colonel Mannheim was watching him, a look of interest on his face, but he said nothing.

"To me," Stanton said, "it seems incredible that the combined intelligence and organizational ability of the UN Government is incapable of finding anything out about one single alien, no matter how competent he may be. Somehow, somewhere, someone must have gotten a line on the Nipe. He must have a base for his operations, and someone should have found it by this time.

"I may be faster and stronger and more sensitive than any other living human being, but that doesn't mean I have superhuman powers, or that I'm a magician. And I'm quite certain that you, Colonel, don't credit me with such abilities. You don't believe that I can do in a short time what the combined forces of the Government couldn't do in ten. Certainly you wouldn't rely too heavily on it.

"And yet, apparently, you are.

"To me, that can only mean that you have another ace up your sleeve. You *know* we're going to get the Nipe fairly quickly. You either have a sure way of tracing him, or you already know where he is.

"Which is it?"

Colonel Mannheim sighed. "We know where he is," he said. "We have known for six years."

6

The Nipe prowled around the huge underground room, carefully checking his alarms. If anyone entered the network of tunnels at any point, the instruments would register that fact. They had to be adjusted, of course, for the presence of the small, omnivorous quadrupeds that ran through the tunnels in such numbers, but anything larger than they would be noted immediately.

He did not like to leave this place. Here, over a period of ten revolutions of this planet about its primary, he had built himself a nest that was almost comfortable. Here, too, were his workshops and his storehouses. He had reason to believe that he was safe here, screened and protected as he was, but each time he left or entered he ran the chance of being observed.

Still, there was no help for it. Thus far, he had been hampered by technical problems. There were things he needed that he could not make for himself. Even his own vast memory, with its every bit of information instantly available, could only contain what had been acquired over a lifetime, and even his long life had not been long enough to acquire every bit of knowledge he needed.

His work had been long and tedious. There were many things that could neither be made in his workshops nor obtained from the natives, things he did not know how to make and which the local species had not yet evolved in their own technology. Or, more likely, which had not been allowed them. In such cases, he had had to make do with other, lesser techniques, which added to the complexity of his job.

But now another problem had intruded itself into his schedule.

He had a name. Colonel Walther Mannheim. The meaning of the verbal symbolism was unknown to him. The patterns of the symbolism were even more evasive than the patterns of the language itself. "Colonel" seemed simple enough. It indicated a certain sociomilitary class that was rigidly defined in one way and very hazy in another. But the meanings and relationships of both "Walther" and "Mannheim" were beyond him. What difference, for instance, was there between a "Walther" and a "William"? Did a "Mannheim" outrank a "Mandeville", or the other way around? What functions differentiated a "John Smith" from a "Peter Taylor"? He knew what a "john" was and what a "smith" was, but "John Smith" was not, apparently, necessarily associated with sanitary plumbing. The meaning of some other names eluded him entirely.

But that made little difference at the moment. The meaning of Colonel Walther Mannheim's symbolic nomenclature was secondary in comparison with his known function.

That required that the Nipe must eventually find and confront Colonel Walther Mannheim.

It meant time lost, of course. It meant that precious time, which should be given to building his communicator, must be given over to what was merely a protective action.

But there was nothing to do but go on. It would never have occurred to the Nipe to give up, for to quit meant to die. And to die-here, now-was unthinkable.

His alarms were all functioning, his defenses all set. He could now leave his hideaway knowing that if it were broken into while he was away he would be warned in time. But he had no real fear of that. He had done everything he could do. And no intelligent creature, to the Nipe's way of thinking, would waste time worrying about a situation he could not improve upon.

Taking with him the equipment he needed for the job he had to do, he entered the tunnel that ran southward from his base of operations. Once, as he moved along, one of the little quadrupeds approached him, its teeth bared. With an almost negligent flip of one powerful, superfast hand, he slammed it against a nearby wall. It dropped and lay still. Another of its kind approached it cautiously. The Nipe noticed the approach with approval. The quadrupeds had no real intelligence, but they had the proper instincts.

At last the Nipe came to another of the many places where the tunnels met with others of the network. He crossed through several rooms, all very large and cluttered with the dusty, long-dead bones of hundreds of the local intelligent life-form —if (and he was not sure in his own mind of this) they could actually be called intelligent. But he moved carefully, stepping over the human bones and the empty, staring skulls. They had apparently been properly devoured, although he could not be sure whether it had been done by their own kind or by the little quadrupeds. Nonetheless, he would not willingly disturb their repose.

He went on into the tunnel that led westward and followed it as it began to angle down. Finally he came to the water's edge.

To a human being, the cold expanse of water that gleamed like ink in the light of the Nipe's illuminator would have been a barricade as impenetrable as steel. But to the Nipe the tidal pool was simply another of his defenses, for it concealed the only entrance he ever used. He went in after adjusting his scuba mask and began swimming toward the opening that led to the estuary of the sea, his eight strong limbs working in unison in a way that would have been the envy of a rowing team.

At the jagged hole in the tunnel wall, the gap that led into open water, he paused to check his instruments. Only after he was certain that there were no sonar or other detector radiations did he propel himself onward, out into the estuary itself.

An hour later, he was warily circling the spot where his little submarine was hidden. He pressed a button on a small device in his hand, and a signal was sent to the submarine. The various devices within it all responded properly. Nothing had been disturbed since the Nipe had set those devices weeks before.

This was the touchiest part of any of his expeditions. There was always the chance, unlikely as it might be, that some one of the bipedal natives had found his machine. He dared not use it too close to his base because of the possibility of its drive vibrations being detected in the narrow estuary. Out here in the open sea there was far less likelihood of that, but leaving his submarine concealed out here increased the danger he exposed himself to every time he left his hidden nest.

Satisfied that the machine was just as he had left it, he entered it and started its engines. He moved slowly and cautiously until he was well out to sea, well away from the continental shelf and over the ocean deeps. Then and only then did he accelerate to full cruising speed.

The full moon was in the west, hiding behind an array of low, scudding clouds, revealing its radiance in fitful bursts of silvery splendor that died again as another clotted cloud moved before the face of the white disk. The shifting light, shining through the breeze-tossed leaves of the palm trees on the beach below, made strange shadows on the sand, ever-changing patterns of gray and black on a background of white, moonlit sand.

But the strangest shadow of all was one that did not change as the others did —a great centipede-like shape that seemed to wash slowly ashore on the receding tide. For a short while, it remained at the water's edge, apparently unmoving in the wash of the waves.

Then, keeping low and balancing himself on his third pair of limbs, the Nipe moved in across the beach. The specially constructed sandals he wore left behind them a set of very human-looking footprints-prints that would remain unnoticed among the myriad of others that were already on the beach, left there by daytime bathers.

It required more time yet to reach the city, and still more time to find the place he was looking for. It was almost dawn before he managed to find a storm sewer in which to hide for the day.

It was partly his difficulty in finding a given spot in a city-almost any city-that had convinced the Nipe that the pseudo-intelligence of the bipeds of this planet could not really be called true intelligence. There was no standardized method of orienting oneself in a city. Not only were no two cities alike in their orientation systems, but the same city would often vary from section to section. Their co-ordinate systems meant almost nothing. Part of a given co-ordinate might be a number, and the rest of it a name, but the meanings of the numbers and names were never the same. It was as though some really intelligent outside agency had given them the basic idea of a co-ordinate system, and they, not having the intelligence to use it properly, had simply jumbled the whole thing up.

That the natives themselves had no real understanding of any such system had long been apparent to him. The dwellers in any one area would naturally be familiar with it; they would know where each place was, regardless of what meaningless names and numbers might be attached to it. But strangers to that area would not know, and could not know. The only thing they could possibly do would be to ask directions of a local citizen-which, the Nipe had learned, was exactly what they did.

Unfortunately, it was not that simple for the Nipe. There was no way for him to walk up to a native and inquire for an address. He had to prowl unseen through the alleys and sewers of a city, picking up a name here, a number there, by eavesdropping on street conversations. He had found that every city contained certain uniformed individuals whose duty it was to direct strangers, and by focusing a directional microphone on such men and listening, it was possible to glean little bits of knowledge that could eventually be co-ordinated into a whole understanding of the city's layout. It was a time-consuming process, but it was the only way the job could be done. Reconnaissance took a tremendous amount of time away from his serious work, but that work could not proceed without materials to work with, and to get those materials required reconnaissance. The dilemma was unavoidable.

And, being what he was, the Nipe accepted the unavoidable and pursued his course with phlegmatic equanimity.

Overhead, the city was beginning to waken. The volume of sound began to increase.

Police Patrolman John Flanders relieved his fellow officer, Patrolman Fred Pilsudski, at a few minutes of eight in the morning.

It was a beautiful day, even for Miami. In the east, the morning sun shone brightly through the hard, transparent pressure glass that covered the street, making the smooth, resilient surface of the street itself glow with warm light. Overhead, Patrolman Flanders could see the aircars in their incessant motion-apparently random, unless one knew what the traffic pattern was and how to look for it. It was Patrolman Flanders' immediate ambition to be promoted to traffic patrol, so that he could be in an aircar above the city instead of watching pedestrians down here on the streets.

"Morning, Fred," he said to his brother officer. "How'd the night go?"

"Hi, Johnny. Pretty good. Not much excitement." He looked at his wristwatch. "You're a couple minutes early yet."

"Yeah. The baby started singing for his breakfast at a God-awful hour. Harriet woke up to feed him, which woke me up, so here I am. If you want to give me the call button, I'll take over. You can go get yourself a cup of coffee."

"I'm up to here with coffee," Pilsudski said, indicating a point just below his left ear. "I'll have a beer instead."

He touched a switch at his belt and said: "Area 37 HQ, this is 13392 Pilsudski."

A voice in his helmet phones said: "37 HQ, go ahead, Pilsudski."

"Time: 0758 hours. I am being relieved by 14278 Flanders."

"Right. Go ahead."

Pilsudski took off the light, strong helmet, reached inside it, opened a small sliding panel, and took out an object the size and shape of an aspirin tablet-the sealed unit that permitted him to understand the conversation over the police wave band. Without it, the police calls would have been gibberish.

Flanders accepted the little gadget from the other officer and inserted it in his own helmet. Then he replaced the helmet on his head. "Area 37 HQ, this is 14278 Flanders. I am relieving 13392 Pilsudski."

"37 HQ," said the voice in his ears. "Okay, Flanders. Transfer recorded."

Police Patrolman John Flanders, Badge Number 14278, was now officially on duty.

He looked up into the sky. "Now there's the place to be on a day like this, Fred. Traffic patrol."

"Not me," said Pilsudski. "Too damn dull. I was on it for six months. Damn near drove me nuts. Nobody to talk to but another cop-same cop, day after day. He was a nice guy, don't get me wrong, but Christ! Nothin' to do but watch for people breakin' traffic pattern. Can't even pull over to the side and watch the traffic go by. It's dull, I'm tellin' you, Johnny. I asked for a transfer back to a beat so's I could see some people again."

"Maybe," said Flanders. "I'd still like to try it."

"Ever'body to their own taste, I guess. Mitchell and Warber were in luck last night, though. Excitement." He sounded as though he meant the word to be sarcastic.

"What happened?" Flanders asked.

"Some boob was having a fight with his wife and his air intake was goofing off at the same time. So, while she's yelling at him, he puts his aircar on hover." He pointed upward. "Right up there, in Level Two. He opens the window of his aircar, mind you. His air intake ain't workin', like I said. Mitchell, in Car 87, spots him and heads for him, figuring there's trouble."

"But no trouble?" asked Flanders.

"Trouble enough. The driver's old lady throws a wrench at him, an' it goes out the window." He chuckled. "First I heard about it was when that damn wrench comes down and bounces off the pressure glass, then up to the side of the building there, and back to the pressure glass. Then it slides off into the rain gutter."

Flanders looked up at the curve of hard, tough, almost invisible pressure glass that covered the street. "With all the cars overhead that we got in this city," Flanders said philosophically, "something like that's bound to happen every so often. That's why that glass is up there, besides for keepin' the rain off your head."

"Yeah," Pilsudski said. "Anyway, Mitchell and Warber got there just as she tossed the wrench. Arrested both of 'em. Now, wasn't that exciting?"

Flanders grinned. "Fred, if the rest of their tour of duty was as dull as you say it was, then I reckon that must have been real exciting."

"Hah." Pilsudski shrugged. "Well, I'm for that beer. See you tomorrow, Johnny."

"Right. Take care o' yourself."

As Pilsudski walked away, Flanders put his hands behind his back, grasping the left in the right. He spread his feet slightly apart. In that time-honored position of the foot patrolman, he surveyed his beat, up and down both sides of the street. Everything looked perfectly normal. Another working day had begun.

He had no idea that he was standing only a few yards from the most hated and feared killer on the face of the Earth.

The only clue that he could possibly have had to that killer's presence was a small ovoid the size and shape of a match head, a dark, dull gray in color, which protruded slightly from a sewer grating six feet away, supported on a hair-thin stalk. In one end was a tiny dark opening, and that opening was pointed directly at Officer Flanders' head. When he began walking slowly down the street, the little ovoid moved, turning slowly on its stalk to keep that dark hole pointed steadily. It was so small, that ovoid, and so inconspicuous, that no one, even looking directly at it, would have noticed it.

The Nipe could see and hear without being either seen or heard himself.

All morning long the tiny ovoid remained in place, watching, listening.

At 11:24 a woman in a cherry-pink dress walked up to Officer Flanders and said: "Pardon me, Officer. Could you tell me where I could find the Donahue Building?"

And while the policeman told her, the Nipe listened carefully. Now he knew what street he was on and its location in respect to two other streets. He also had a number. He remembered them all, accurately and completely. It was a good beginning, he decided. It would not be too long before he would have enough to enable him to locate the address he was looking for. After that, there would only remain the job of observing and making plans to get what he wanted at that address.

He settled himself to wait for more information. He knew that it would be a long wait.

But he was prepared for that.

SECOND INTERLUDE

The woman's eyes were filled with tears, for which the doctor was privately thankful. At least, he thought to himself, the original shock has worn off.

"And there's nothing we can do?" she asked. "Nothing?" There was anguish in her voice.

"I'm afraid not," the doctor told her gently. "Not yet. There are research men working on the problem, and one day ... perhaps ..." Then he shook his head. "But not yet." He paused. "I'm sorry, Mrs. Stanton."

The woman sat there in the comfortable chair and looked at the specialist's diploma on the doctor's wall-and yet, she really didn't see the diploma at all. She was seeing something else —a kind of dream that had been shattered.

After a moment, she began to speak, her voice low and gentle, as though the dream were still going on and she were half afraid she might waken herself if she spoke too loudly.

"Jim and I were so glad they were twins. Identical twin boys. He said ... I remember, he said, 'We ought to call them Ike and Mike.' And he laughed a little when he said it, to show he didn't mean it."

The doctor said nothing, waiting for her to go on.

"I remember, I was propped up in the bed, the afternoon after they were born, and Jim brought me a new bed jacket, and I said I didn't need a new one because I'd be going right home the very next day, and he said, 'Hell, kid, you don't think I'd buy a bed jacket just for hospital use, now do you? This is for breakfasts in bed, too.'

"And that's when he said he'd seen the boys and said we ought to name them Ike and Mike."

The tears were coming down Mrs. Stanton's cheeks heavily now, and the grief made her look older than her twenty-four years, but the doctor said nothing, letting her spill out her emotions in words.

"We'd talked about it before, you know-soon as the obstetrician found out that I was going to have twins. And Jim ... Jim said that we shouldn't name them alike unless they were identical twins or mirror twins. If they were fraternal twins, we'd just name them as if they'd been ordinary brothers or sisters or whatever. You know?" She looked at the doctor, her eyes pleading for understanding.

"I know," he said.

"And Jim was always kidding. If they were girls, he said, we ought to call them Flora and Dora, or Annie and Fanny, or maybe Susie and Floozie. He was always kidding about it. You know?"

"I know," said the doctor.

"And then ... and then when they *were* identical boys, he was very sensible about it. He was always so sensible. 'We'll call them Martin and Bartholomew,' he said. 'Then if they want to call themselves Mart and Bart, they can, but they won't be stuck with any rhyming names if they don't want them.' Jim was always very thoughtful that way, Doctor. Very thoughtful."

She seemed suddenly to realize that she was crying and took a handkerchief out of her sleeve to dab at her eyes and face.

"I'll have to quit crying," she said, trying to sound very brave and very strong. "After all, it could have been worse, couldn't it? I mean, the radiation could have killed my boy, too. Jim's dead, yes, and I've got to get used to that. But I still have two boys to take care of, and they'll need me."

"Yes, Mrs. Stanton, they will," said the doctor. "They'll both need you very much. And you'll have to be very gentle and very careful with both of them."

"How ... how do you mean that?" she asked.

The doctor settled back in his chair and chose his words carefully. "Identical twins tend to identify with each other, Mrs. Stanton. There is a great deal of empathy between people who are not only of the same age, but genetically identical. If they were both completely healthy, there would normally be very little trouble in their education at home or in school. Any of

33

the standard texts on psychodynamics in education will show you the pitfalls to avoid when dealing with identical siblings.

"But your sons are no longer identical, Mrs. Stanton. One is normal, healthy, and lively. The other is ... well, as you know, he is slow, sluggish, and badly co-ordinated. The condition may improve with time, but, until we know more about such damage than we do now, he will remain an invalid."

He had been watching her for further signs of emotional upset. But she seemed to be listening calmly enough. He went on.

"That's the trouble with radiation damage, Mrs. Stanton. Even when we can save the victim's life, we cannot always save his health.

"You can see, I think, what sort of psychic disturbances this might bring about in such a pair. The ill boy tends to identify with the well one, and, oddly enough, the reverse is also true. If they are not properly handled during their formative years, Mrs. Stanton, both can be badly damaged emotionally."

"I ... I think I understand, Doctor," the young woman said. "But what sort of thing should I look out for? What sort of things should I avoid?"

"First off, I suggest you get a good man in psychic development," the doctor said. "I, myself, would hesitate to prescribe. It's out of my field. But I can say that, in general, most of your trouble will be caused by a tendency for the pair to swing into one of two extremes.

"At one extreme, you will have mutual antagonism. This arises when the ill child becomes jealous of the other's health, while, on the other hand, the healthy one becomes jealous of the extra consideration that is shown to his crippled brother.

"At the other extreme, the healthy boy may identify so closely with his brother that he feels every slight or hurt, real or imagined, which the ill boy is subjected to. He becomes extremely over-solicitous, over-protective. At the same time, the invalid brother may come to depend completely on his healthy twin.

"In both these situations there is a positive feedback that constantly worsens the condition. It requires a great deal of careful observation and careful application of the proper educational stimuli to keep the situation from developing toward either extreme. You'll need expert help if you want both boys to display the full abilities of which they are potentially capable."

"I see," the woman said. "Could you give me the name of a good man, Doctor?"

The doctor nodded and picked up a book on his desk. "I'll give you the names of several. You can pick the one you like best, the one with whom you seem to be most comfortable. Try several or all of them before you decide. They're all good men. There are many good women in the field, too, but in this case I think a man would be best. Of course, if one of them thinks a woman is indicated, that's up to him. As I said, that isn't my field."

He opened the small book and riffled through it to find the names he wanted.

7

The image of the Nipe on the glowing screen was clear and finely detailed. It was, Stanton thought, as though one were looking through a window into the Nipe's nest itself. Only the tremendous depth of focus of the lens that had caught the picture gave the illusion a feeling of unreality. Everything-background and foreground alike-was sharply in focus.

Like some horrendous dream monster, the Nipe moved in slow motion, giving Stanton the eerie feeling that the alien was moving through a thicker, heavier medium than air, in a place where the gravity was much less than that of Earth. With ponderous deliberation, the fingers of one of his hands closed upon the handle of an oddly shaped tool and lifted it slowly from the surface upon which he worked.

"That's our best-placed camera," said Colonel Mannheim, "but some of the others can always get details that this one doesn't. The trouble is that we'll never really have enough cameras in there-not unless we stud the walls, ceilings, and floors with them, and even then I'm not so sure we'd get everything. It isn't the same as having a trained expert on camera who is *trying* to demonstrate what he's doing. An expert plays to the camera and never obstructs any of his own movements. But the Nipe ..." He left the sentence unfinished and shook his head sadly.

Stanton narrowed his eyes at the image. To his own speeded-up perceptive processes, the motion seemed intolerably slow. "Would you mind speeding it up a little?" he asked the colonel. "I want to get an idea of the way he moves, and I can't really get the feeling of it at this speed."

"Certainly." The colonel turned to the technician at the controls. "Speed the tape up to normal. If there's anything Mr. Stanton wants to look at more closely, we can run it through again."

As if in obedience to the colonel's command, the Nipe seemed to shake himself a little and go about his business more briskly, and the air and gravity seemed to revert to those of Earth.

"What's he doing?" Stanton asked. The Nipe was performing some sort of operation on an odd-looking box that sat on the floor in front of him.

The colonel pointed. "He's got a screwdriver that he's modified to give it a head with an L-shaped cross section, and he's wiggling it around inside that hole in the box. But what he's doing is a secret between God and the Nipe at this point," Colonel Mannheim said glumly.

Stanton glanced away from the screen for a moment to look at the other men who were there. Some of them were watching the screen, but most of them seemed to be watching Stanton, although they looked away as soon as they saw his eyes on them. All, that is, except Dr. George Yoritomo, who simply gave him a smile of confidence.

Trying to see what kind of a bloke this touted superman is, Stanton thought. *Well, I can't say I blame 'em.*

He brought his attention back to the screen.

So this was the Nipe's hideaway. He wondered if it were furnished in the fashion that a Nipe's living quarters would be furnished on whatever planet the multilegged horror had come from. Probably it had the same similarity as Robinson Crusoe's island home had to a middle-class nineteenth-century English home.

There was no furniture in it at all, as such. Low-slung as he was, the Nipe needed no tables or workbenches; all his work was spread out on the floor, with a neatness and tidiness that would have surprised many human technicians. For the same reason, he needed no chairs, and, since true sleep was a form of metabolic rest he evidently found unnecessary, he needed no bed. The closest thing he did that might be called sleep was his habit of stopping whatever he was doing and remaining quiet for periods of time that ranged from a few minutes to a couple of hours. Sometimes his eyes remained opened during these periods, sometimes they were closed. It was difficult to tell whether he was sleeping or just thinking.

"The difficulty was in getting cameras in there in the first place," Colonel Mannheim was saying. "That's why we missed so much of his early work. There! Look at that!" His finger jabbed at the image.

"The attachment he's making?"

"That's right. Now, it looks as though it's a meter of some kind, but we don't know whether it's a test instrument or an integral and necessary part of the machine he's making. The whole machine might even be only a test instrument for something else he's building. Or perhaps a machine to make parts for some other machine. After all, he had to start out from the very beginning–making the tools to make the tools to make the tools, you know."

Dr. Yoritomo spoke for the first time. "It's not quite as bad as all that, eh, Colonel? We must remember that he had our technology to draw upon. If he'd been wrecked on Earth two or three centuries ago, he wouldn't have been able to do a thing."

Colonel Mannheim smiled at the tall, lean man. "Granted," he said agreeably, "but it's quite obvious that there are parts of our technology that are just as alien to him as parts of his are to us. Remember how he went to all the trouble of building a pentode vacuum tube for a job that could have been done by transistors he already had had a chance to get and didn't. His knowledge of solid-state physics seems to be about a century and a half behind ours."

Stanton listened. Dr. Yoritomo was, in effect, one of his training instructors. *Advanced Alien Psychology*, Stanton thought; *Seminar Course. The Mental Whys & Wherefores of the Nipe, or How to Outthink the Enemy in Twelve Dozen Easy Lessons. Instructor: Dr. George Yoritomo.*

The smile on Yoritomo's face was beatific, but he held up a warning finger. "Ah, ah, Colonel! We mustn't fall into a trap like that so easily. Remember that gimmick he built last year? The one that blinded those people in Baghdad? It had five perfect emeralds in it, connected in series with silver wire. Eh?"

"That's true," the colonel admitted. "But they weren't used the way we'd use semiconducting materials."

"Indeed not. But the thing *worked*, didn't it? He has a knowledge of solid-state physics that we don't have, and vice versa."

"Which one would you say was ahead of the other?" Stanton asked. "I don't mean just in solid-state physics, but in science as a whole."

"That's a difficult question to answer," Dr. Yoritomo said thoughtfully. "Frankly, I'd put my money on his technology as encompassing more than ours–at least, insofar as the physical sciences are concerned."

"I agree," said Colonel Mannheim. "He's got things in that little nest of his that —" He stopped and shook his head slowly, as though he couldn't find words.

"I will say this," Yoritomo continued. "Whatever his great technological abilities, our friend the Nipe has plenty of good, solid guts. And patience." He smiled a little, and then amended his statement. "From our own point of view."

Stanton looked at him quizzically. "How do you mean? I was just about to agree with you until you tacked that last phrase on. What does point of view have to do with it?"

"Everything, I should say," said Yoritomo. "It all depends on the equipment an individual has. A man, for instance, who rushes into a building to save a life, wearing nothing but street clothes, has courage. A man who does the same thing when he's wearing a nullotherm suit is an unknown quantity. There is no way of knowing, from that action alone, whether he has courage or not."

Stanton thought he saw what the scientist was driving at. "But you're not talking about technological equipment now," he said.

"Not at all. I'm talking about personal equipment." He turned his head slightly to look at the colonel. "Colonel Mannheim, do you think it would require any personal courage on Mr. Stanton's part to stand up against you in a face-to-face gunfight?"

The colonel grinned tightly. "I see what you mean."

Stanton grinned back rather wryly. "So do I. No, it wouldn't."

"On the other hand," Yoritomo continued, "if you were to challenge Mr. Stanton, would that show courage on your part, Colonel?"

"Not really. Foolhardiness, stupidity or insanity–but not courage."

"Ah, then," said Yoritomo with a beaming smile, "neither of you can prove you have guts enough to fight the other. Can you?"

Mannheim smiled grimly and said nothing. But Stanton was thinking the whole thing out very carefully. "Just a second," he said. "That depends on the circumstances. If Colonel Mannheim, say, knew that forcing me to shoot him would save the life of someone more important than himself-or, perhaps, the lives of a great many people-what then?"

Yoritomo bowed his head in a quick nod. "Exactly. That is what I meant by viewpoint. Whether the Nipe has courage or patience or any other human feeling depends on two things: his own abilities and exactly how much information he has. A man can perform any action without fear if he knows that it will not hurt him-or if he does *not* know that it *will*."

Stanton thought that over in silence.

The image of the Nipe was no longer moving. He had settled down into his "sleeping position" —unmoving, although the baleful violet eyes were still open. "Cut that off," Colonel Mannheim said to the operator. "There's not much to learn from the rest of that tape."

As the image blanked out, Stanton said, "Have you actually managed to build any of the devices he's constructed, Colonel?"

"Some," said Colonel Mannheim. "We have specialists all over the world studying those tapes. We have the advantage of being able to watch every step the Nipe makes, and we know the materials he's been using to work with. But, even so, the scientists are baffled by many of them. Can you imagine the time James Clerk Maxwell would have had trying to build a modern television set from tapes like this?"

"I can imagine," Stanton said.

"You can see, then, why we're depending on you," Mannheim said.

Stanton merely nodded. The knowledge that he was actually a focal point in human history, that the whole future of the human race depended to a tremendous extent on him, was a realization that weighed heavily and, at the same time, was immensely bracing.

"And now," the colonel said, "I'll turn you over to Dr. Yoritomo. He'll be able to give you a great deal more information than I can."

8

The girl moved with the peculiar gliding walk so characteristic of a person walking under low-gravity conditions, and the ease and grace with which she did it showed that she was no stranger to low-gee. To the three men from Earth who followed her a few paces behind, the gee-pull seemed so low as to be almost nonexistent, although it was actually a shade over one quarter of that of Earth, the highest gravitational pull of any planetoid in the Belt. Their faint feeling of nausea was due simply to their lack of experience with *really* low gravity-the largest planetoid in the Belt had a surface gravity that was only one eighth of the pull they were now experiencing, and only one thirty-second of the Earth gravity they were used to.

The planetoid they were on-or rather, *in* —was known throughout the Belt simply as Thread-needle Street, and was nowhere near as large as Ceres. What accounted for the relatively high gravity pull of this tiny body was its spin. Moving in its orbit, out beyond the orbit of Mars, it turned fairly rapidly on its axis-rapidly enough to overcome the feeble gravitational field of its mass. It was a solid, roughly spherical mass of nickel-iron, nearly two thirds of a mile in diameter and, like the other inhabited planetoids of the Belt, honeycombed with corridors and rooms cut out of the living metal itself. But the corridors and rooms were oriented differently from those of the other planetoids; Threadneedle Street made one complete rotation about its axis in something less than a minute and a half, and the resulting centrifugal force reversed the normal "up" and "down", so that the center of the planetoid was overhead to anyone walking inside it. It was that fact which added to the queasiness of the three men from Earth who were following the girl down the corridor. They knew that only a few floors beneath them yawned the mighty nothingness of infinite space.

The girl, totally unconcerned with thoughts of that vast emptiness, stopped before a door that led off the corridor and opened it. "Mr. Martin," she said, "these are the gentlemen who have an appointment with you. Mr. Gerrol. Mr. Vandenbosch. Mr. Nguma." She called off each name as the man bearing it walked awkwardly through the door. "Gentlemen," she finished, "this is Mr. Stanley Martin." Then she left, discreetly closing the door.

The young man behind the desk in the metal-walled office stood up smiling as the three men entered, offered his hand to each, and shook hands warmly. "Sit down, gentlemen," he said, gesturing toward three solidly built chairs that had been anchored magnetically to the nickel-iron floor of the room.

"Well," he said genially when the three had seated themselves, "how was the trip out?"

He watched them closely, without appearing to do so, as they made their polite responses to his question. He was acquainted with them only through correspondence; now was his first chance to evaluate them in person.

Barnabas Nguma, a very tall man whose dark brown skin and eyes made a sharp contrast with the white of the mass of tiny, crisp curls on his head, smiled when he spoke, but there were lines of worry etched around his eyes. "Pleasant enough, Mr. Martin. I'm afraid that steady one-gee acceleration has left me unprepared for this low gravity."

"Well," said Stefan Vandenbosch, "it really isn't so bad, once you get used to it. As long as it's steady, I don't mind it." He was a rather chubby man of average height, with blond hair that was beginning to gray at the temples and pale blue eyes that gave his face an expression of almost childlike innocence.

Arthur Gerrol, the third man, was almost as light-complexioned as Vandenbosch. His thinning hair was light brown, and his eyes were a deep gray-blue, and the lines in his hard, blocky face gave him a look of grim determination. "I agree, Stefan. It isn't the low gravity *per se*. It's the doggone surges. We went from one gee to zero when the ship came in for a landing at the pole of Threadneedle Street. Then, as we came back down here, the gravity kept going up, and that ...what do you call it? Coriolis force? Yeah, that's it. It made my head feel as though the whole room was spinning." Then, realizing what he'd said, he laughed sharply.

The man behind the desk laughed with him. "Yes, it is a bit disconcerting at first, but the spin gives enough gee-pull to make a man feel comfortable, once he's used to it. That's one of the reasons why Threadneedle Street was picked. As the financial center of the Belt, we have a great many visitors from Earth, and one-quarter gee is a lot easier to get used to than a fiftieth." Then he looked quickly at the others and said, "Now, gentlemen, how can Lloyd's of London help you?"

He had phrased it that way on purpose, deliberately making it awkward for them to bring up the subject they had on their minds.

It was Nguma who broke the short silence. "Quite simply, Mr. Martin, we have come to put our case before you in person. It is not Lloyd's want-it is you."

"You refer to our correspondence on the Nipe case, Mr. Nguma?"

"Exactly. We feel —"

The man behind the desk interrupted him. "Mr. Nguma, do you have any further information?" He looked as though such news would be welcome but that it would not change his mind in the least.

"That's just it, Mr. Martin," said Nguma, "we don't know whether our little bits and dribbles of information are worth anything."

The man behind the desk leaned back in his chair again. "I see," he said softly. "Well, just what is it you want of me, Mr. Nguma?"

Nguma looked surprised. "Why, just what I've written, sir! You are acknowledged as the greatest detective in the Solar System-bar none. We need you, Mr. Martin! *Earth* needs you! That inhuman monster has been killing and robbing for ten years! Men, women, and children have been slaughtered and eaten as though they were cattle! You've *got* to help us find that God-awful thing!"

Before there could be any answer, Arthur Gerrol leaned forward earnestly and said, "Mr. Martin, we don't just represent businessmen who have been robbed. We also represent hundreds and hundreds of people who have had friends and relatives murdered by that horror. Little people, Mr. Martin. Ordinary people who are helpless against the terror of a superhuman evil. This isn't just a matter of money and goods lost-it's a matter of *lives* lost. Human lives, Mr. Martin."

"They're not the only ones who are concerned, either," Vandenbosch broke in. "If that hellish thing isn't destroyed, more will die. Who knows how long a beast like that may live? What is its life-span? Nobody knows!" He waved a hand in the air. "For all we know, it could go on for another century-maybe more-killing, killing, killing."

The detective looked at them for a moment in silence. These three men represented more than just a group of businessmen who had grown uneasy about the Government's ability to catch the Nipe; they represented more than a few hundred or even a few thousand people who had been directly affected by the monster's depredations. They represented the growing feeling of unrest that was making itself known all over Earth. It was even making itself felt out here in the Belt, although the Nipe had not, in the past decade, shown any desire to leave Earth. Why hadn't the beast been found? Why couldn't it be killed? Why were its raids always so fantastically successful?

For every toothmark that inhuman thing had left on a human bone, it had left a thousand on human minds-marks of a fear that was more than a fear. It was a deep-seated terror of the unknown.

The number of people killed in ordinary accidents in a single week was greater than the total number killed by the Nipe in the last decade, but nowhere were men banding together to put a stop to that sort of death. Accidental death was a known factor, almost a friend; the Nipe was stark horror.

The detective said: "Gentlemen, I'm sorry, but what I said in my last letter still goes. I can't take the job. I will not go to Earth."

Every one of the three men could sense the determination in his voice, the utter finality of his words. There was no mistaking the iron-hard will of the man. They knew that nothing could shake him-nothing, at least, that they could do.

But they couldn't admit defeat. No matter how futile they knew it to be, they still had to try.

Nguma took a billfold from his jacket pocket, opened it, and took out an engraved sheet of paper with an embossed seal in one corner. He put it on the desk in front of the detective.

"Would you look at that, Mr. Martin?" he asked.

The detective picked it up and looked at it. The expression on his face did not change. "Two hundred and fifty thousand," he said, in a voice that showed only polite interest. "A cool quarter of a million. That's a lot of money, Mr. Nguma."

"It is," said Nguma. "As you can see, that sum has just been deposited here, in the Belt branch of the Bank of England. It will be transferred to your account immediately, as soon as you agree to come to Earth to find and kill the Nipe."

The detective looked up from his inspection of the certificate. He had known that the three men had made a visit to the Bank's offices, and he had been fairly sure of their purpose when he had received the information. He had not known the sum would be quite so large.

"A quarter of a million, just to take the job?" he asked. "And what if I don't catch him?"

"We have faith in you, Mr. Martin," Nguma said. "We know your reputation. We know what you've done in the past. The Government police haven't been able to do anything. They're completely baffled, and have been for ten years. They will continue to be so. This alien's mind is too devilishly sharp for the kind of men in Government service. We know that when you take this job the finest brain in the Solar System will be searching for that horror. If you can't find him ..." He spread his hands in a gesture that was partly a dismissal of all hope and partly an appeal to the man whose services he wanted so desperately.

The detective put the certificate down on the desk top and pushed it toward Nguma. "That's very flattering, sir. Really. And I wish there were some more diplomatic way of saying no-but that's all I can say."

"There will be a like sum deposited to your account as soon as you either kill or capture the Nipe, or, discovering his hideout, enable the Government officials to kill or capture him," said Nguma.

"That's half a million in all," Gerrol put in. "We've worked hard to raise that money, Mr. Martin. It should be enough."

The detective kept his temper under icy control, allowing just enough of his anger to show to make his point. "Mr. Gerrol ...it is not a question of money. Your offer is more than generous."

"It's our final offer," Gerrol said flatly.

"I hope it is, Mr. Gerrol," the detective said coldly. "I sincerely hope it is. For the past six months, you and your organization have been trying to get me to take this job. I appreciate the sincerity of your efforts, believe me. And, as I said, I am honored and flattered that you should think so highly of me. On the other hand, your method of going about it is hardly flattering. I turned down your first offer of twenty thousand six months ago. Since then, you have been going up and up and up until you have finally reached twenty-five times the original amount. You seem to think I have been holding out for more money. I have attempted to disabuse you of that notion, but you would not read what I put down in my communications, evidently. If I had wanted more money than you offered at first, I would have said so. I would have quoted you a price. I did not. I gave you an unqualified refusal. I give it to you still. *No.* Flatly, absolutely, and finally ... *no.*"

Nguma was the only one of the three who could find his tongue immediately. "I should think," he said somewhat acidly, "that you would consider it your duty to —"

The detective cut him off. "My duty, Mr. Nguma, is, at this moment, to my employers. I am a paid investigator for Lloyd's of London, Belt branch. I draw a salary that is more than adequate for my needs and almost adequate for my taste in the little luxuries of life. I am, for the time being at least, satisfied with my work. So are my employers. Until one or the other of us becomes dissatisfied, the situation will remain as it is. I will not accept any outside work of any kind except at the instructions of, or with the permission of, my employers. I have neither. I want neither at this time. That is all, gentlemen. Good day."

"But the money ..." Nguma said.

"The money should be withdrawn from the bank and returned to Earth. I suggest you return it to the people who have donated it to your organization. If that is impossible, I suggest you donate it to the Government officials who are working so hard to do the job you want done. I assure you, they are much more capable than I of dealing with the Nipe. Good day, Mr. Nguma, Mr. Vandenbosch, Mr. Gerrol."

They looked hurt, bewildered, and angry. Only Mr. Barnabas Nguma looked as if he might have some slight understanding of what had happened. He was the only one who spoke. "Good day, Mr. Martin. I am sorry we have disturbed you. Thank you for your valuable time," he said with dignity. And then the three men walked out the door, closing it behind them.

The detective sat behind his desk, looking at the door, almost as if he could see the men beyond it as they moved down the corridor. Several minutes later, when his secretary opened the door again, he was still staring thoughtfully at it. She thought he was staring at her.

"Something the matter, Mr. Martin?" she asked.

"What? Oh. No, no. Nothing, Helen; nothing. Just wool-gathering. Did you see our visitors out all right?"

She glided in and closed the door behind her. "Well, none of them fell and broke a leg, if that's what you mean. But that Mr. Gerrol looked as though he might break a blood vessel. I take it you turned them down again?"

"Yes. For the last time, I think. It's a shame they had to travel out here, all that distance, to be turned down. They looked on me as their great white hope. They couldn't really believe I would turn them down. Couldn't let themselves believe it, I guess. They're scared, Helen-bright green scared."

"I know. But if it weren't for the fact that I have certain pretensions to being a lady, I would have booted that Gerrol into orbit without a spacesuit."

"Oh?"

"He implied," Helen said angrily, "that you were a coward. That you were afraid to face the Nipe."

The detective chuckled. "I hope you didn't say anything."

"I wanted to," she admitted. "I wanted to tell him that guns were easy to buy, that all he had to do was buy one and go after the Nipe himself. I would like to have seen his face if I'd asked him how scared *he* was of the beast. But I didn't say a word. They weren't talking to me, anyway; they were talking to each other."

"I'd almost be willing to bet that Nguma disagreed with Gerrol. Nguma didn't think I was a physical coward; he thought I was a moral coward."

"How'd you know?"

"Intuition. Just from the way he talked and acted. He felt the failure more than the others because he felt that there was no hope left at all. He was quite certain that I, myself, did not believe the Nipe could be caught-by me or anyone else. He thinks that I turned down the job because I know I'd fail and I don't want to have a failure on my record. Not *that* big a failure."

"That's ridiculous, of course," the girl said angrily.

The detective noticed a faint note in her voice. *She thinks the same as Nguma,* he thought, *but she doesn't want to admit it to herself.* He massaged his closed eyes with the tips of his fingers. *Maybe she's right,* he thought. *Maybe they're both right.* Aloud, he said, "Well, we've had our little diversion. Let's get back to work."

"Yes, sir. You want the BenChaim file again?"

"Yes. I've got to figure that tricky line down to a T, or we may never see that boy again. We haven't much time, either-two weeks at most."

She went over to the file cabinet and took out several heavy folders. "Imagine," she said, almost to herself, "imagine them trying to get you away from here when you have a kidnap case to solve. They must be out of their minds."

There was no kidnap case six months ago, the detective thought. *She knows that's not the reason. She's only trying to convince herself. Why did I turn them down?*

His mind veered away from the dangerous subject, and for a moment his mental processes refused to focus on anything at all.

The girl put the files down on his desk.

"Thanks, Helen. Now, let's see ..." *I'll work on this*, he thought. *I won't even think about the other at all.*

9

Colonel Walther Mannheim tapped with one thick finger the map that glowed on the wall before him. "That's his nest," he said firmly. "Right there, where those tunnels come together."

Bart Stanton looked at the map of Manhattan Island and at the gleaming colored traceries that threaded their various ways across it. "Just what was the purpose of all those tunnels?" he asked.

"The majority of them were for rail transportation," said the colonel. "The island was hit by a sun bomb during the Holocaust and was almost completely leveled and slagged down. When the city was completely rebuilt afterwards, there was naturally no need for such things, so they were simply all sealed off and forgotten."

"He's hiding directly under Government City," Stanton said. "Incredible."

"It used to be one of the largest seaports in the world," Colonel Mannheim said, "and it very probably still would be if the inertia drive hadn't made air travel cheaper and easier than seagoing."

"How did he find out about those tunnels?" Stanton asked.

The colonel pointed at the north end of the island. "After the Holocaust, the first returnees to the island were wild animals which crossed over from the mainland to the north. The Harlem River isn't very wide at this point, as you can see. There was a bridge right at about this point here-the very tip of the island. It had collapsed into the water, but there was enough of it to allow animals to cross. Because of the rocky hills at this end of the island, there were places which were spared the direct effects of the bomb, and grasses and trees began growing there. That's why it was decided that section should be left as a game preserve when the Government built the capital on the southern part of the island." His finger moved down the map. "The upper three miles of the island, down to here, where it begins to widen, are all game preserve. There's a high wall at this point which separates it from the city, which keeps the animals penned in, and the ruins of the bridges which connected with the mainland have been removed, so animals can't get across any more.

"Two years after he arrived, the Nipe was almost caught. He had managed to get here from Asia by stealing a flyer in Leningrad. According to Dr. Yoritomo and the other psychologists who have been studying the Nipe, he apparently does not believe that human beings are anything more than trained animals. He was looking then-as he is apparently still looking-for the 'real' rulers of Earth. He expected to find them, of course, in Government City. Needless to say," said the colonel with a touch of irony, "he failed."

"But he was seen?" asked Stanton.

"He was seen. And pursued. But he got away easily, heading north. The whole island was searched, from the southern tip to the wall, and the police were ready to start an inch-by-inch combing of the game preserve by the end of the third day after he was seen. But he hit and robbed a chemical supply house in northern Pennsylvania, killing two men, so the search was called off.

"It wasn't until two years later, after an exhaustive analysis of the pattern of his raids had given us enough material to work with, that we determined that he must have found an opening into one of the tunnels up here in the game preserve." He gestured again at the map. "Very likely he immediately saw that no human being had been down there in a long time and that there wasn't much chance of a man coming down there in the foreseeable future. It was a perfect place for his base."

"How does he move in and out?" Stanton asked.

"This way." The colonel traced a finger down one of the red lines on the map, southward, until he came to a spot only a little over two miles from the southernmost tip of the island. The line turned abruptly toward the western shore of the island, where it stopped. "There are tunnels that go underneath the Hudson River at this point and emerge on the other side, over here, in New Jersey. The one he uses is only one of several, but it has one distinct advantage that the others do not. All of them are flooded now; the sun bomb caved them in when the primary shock wave hit the surface of the water. The tunnel he uses has a hole in it big enough for him to swim through.

"In spite of his high rate of metabolism, the Nipe can store a tremendous amount of oxygen in his body and can stay underwater for as long as half an hour without breathing apparatus, if he conserves his energy. When he's wearing his scuba mask, he's practically a self-contained submarine. The pressure doesn't seem to bother him much. He's a tough cookie."

"I'll remember that," said Stanton somberly. "I won't try to race him underwater."

"No," said Colonel Mannheim. "No, I wouldn't do that if I were you."

They both knew that there was a great deal more to it than that. In spite of the near miracle that the staff of the Neurophysical Institute had wrought upon Stanton's nerves and muscles and glands, they could only go so far. They could only improve the functioning of the equipment that Stanton already had; they could not add more.

His lungs could be, and had been, increased tremendously in efficiency of operation, but the amount of air they could actually hold could only be increased slightly. There was no way to add much extra volume to them without doing so at the expense of other organs. In a breath-holding contest, the Nipe would win easily, since his body had evolved organs for oxygen storage, while the human body had not.

You cannot make a silk purse out of a sow's ear if you are limited to the structures and compounds found in sows' ears. The best you can do is make a finer, stronger, more sensitive sow's ear.

"I understand that the Nipe has his hideout pretty well bugged with all kinds of alarms," Stanton said. "How did you get your own bugs in there without setting off his?"

"Well, at first we didn't know for sure what he was up to; we weren't even sure he was actually down in those tunnels. But we suspected that if he was he'd have alarms set all over the place-perhaps even alarms of types we couldn't recognize. But we had to take that chance. We *had* to watch him."

He walked over to the nearby table and opened a box some twelve inches long and five-by-five inches in cross-section.

"See this?" he said, as he took a furry object from the box.

It looked like a large rat. Dead, stiff, unmoving.

"Our spy," said Colonel Mannheim.

The rat moved along the rusted steel rail that ran the length of the huge tunnel. To a human being, the tunnel would have seemed to be in utter darkness, but the little eyes of the rat saw the surroundings as faintly luminescent, glowing from the infra-red radiations given out by the internal warmth of the cement and steel. The main source of the radiations was from above, where the heat of the sun and the warmth from the energy sources in the buildings on the surface seeped through the roof of the tunnel. But here and there were even brighter spots of warmth, spots that moved about on glowing feet and sniffed blindly at the air with tiny glowing noses. Rats.

On and on moved the rat, its little pinkish feet pattering almost silently on the oxidized metal surface of the rails. Its sensitive ears picked up the movements and the squeals of other rats, but it paid them no heed. Several times it met other rats on the rail, but most of them sensed the alienness of *this* rat and scuttled out of its way.

Once, it met a rat who did not give way. Hungry, perhaps, or perhaps merely yielding to the paranoid fury that was a normal component of the rattish mind, it squealed its defiance to the rat that was not a rat. It advanced, baring its rodent teeth in a yellow-daggered snarl of hate.

The rat that was not a rat became suddenly motionless, its sharp little nose pointed directly at the oncoming enemy. There came a noise, a tiny popping hiss, like that of a very small drop of water striking hot metal. From the left nostril of the not-rat, a tiny, glasslike needle snapped out at bullet speed. It struck the advancing rat in the center of the pink tongue that was visible in the open mouth. Then the not-rat scuttled backward faster than any real rat could have moved.

For a second the real rat hesitated, and it may be that the realization penetrated into its dim brain that rats did not fight this way. Then, as the tiny needle dissolved in its bloodstream, it closed its eyes and collapsed, rolling limply off the rail to the rotted wooden tie beneath.

The rat might come to before it was found and devoured by its fellows-or it might not. The not-rat moved on, not caring either way. The human intelligence that looked out from the eyes of the not-rat was only concerned with getting to the Nipe.

"That's how we found the Nipe," Colonel Mannheim said, "and that's how we keep tabs on him now. We have over seven hundred of these remote-control robots hidden in strategic spots throughout those tunnels now, and we can put more in whenever we want, but it took time to get everything set up this way. Now we can follow the Nipe wherever he goes, so long as he stays in those tunnels. If he went out through the one open-air exit up in the northern part of the island, we could have him followed by bird-robots. But" —he shrugged wryly —"I'm afraid the underwater problem still has us stumped. We can't get the carrier wave for the remote-control impulses to go very far underwater."

"How do you get your carrier wave underground to those tunnels?" Stanton asked. "And how do you keep the Nipe from picking up the radiation?"

The colonel grinned widely. "One of the boys dreamed up a real cute gimmick. Those old steel rails themselves act as antennas for the broadcaster, and the rat's tail is the pickup antenna. As long as the rat is crawling right on the rail, only a microscopic amount of power is needed for control, not enough for the Nipe to pick up with his instruments. Each rat carries its own battery for motive power, and there are old copper power cables down there that we can send direct current through to recharge the batteries. And, when we need them, the copper cables can be used as antennas. It took us quite a while to work the system out, but it's running smoothly now."

Stanton rubbed his head thoughtfully. *Damn these gaps in my memory!* he thought. It was sometimes embarrassing to ask questions that any schoolboy should know the answers to.

"Aren't there ways of detecting objects underwater?" he asked after a moment.

"Yes," said the colonel, "several of them. But they all require beamed energy of some kind to be reflected from the object we want to look at, and we don't dare use anything like that." He sat down on one corner of the table, his bright blue eyes looking up at Stanton.

"That's been our big problem all along," he said seriously. "We have to keep the Nipe from knowing he's being watched. In the tunnels themselves, we've only used equipment that was already there, adding only what we absolutely had to-small things. A few strands of wire, a tiny relay, things that can be hidden in out-of-the-way places and can be made to look as though they were a part of the original old equipment. After all, he has his own alarm system in that maze of tunnels, and we have deliberately kept away from his detecting devices. He knows about the rats and ignores them. They're part of the environment. But we don't dare use anything that would tip him off to our knowledge of his whereabouts. One slip like that, and hundreds of human beings will have died in vain."

"And if he stays down there too long," Stanton said levelly, "millions more may die."

The colonel's face was grim as he looked directly into Stanton's eyes. "That's why you have to know your job down to the most minute detail when the time comes to act. The whole success of the plan will depend on you and you alone."

Stanton's eyes didn't avoid the colonel's. *That's not true,* he thought, *I'll be only one man on a team. And you know that, Colonel Mannheim. But you'd like to shove all the responsibility off onto someone else-someone stronger. You've finally met someone that you consider your superior in that way, and you want to unload. I wish I felt as confident as you do ... but I don't.*

Aloud, he said: "Sure. Nothing to it. All I have to do is take into account everything that's known about the Nipe and make allowances for everything that's not known." Then he smiled. "Not," he added, "that I can think of any other way to go about it."

THIRD INTERLUDE

Mrs. Frobisher touched the control button that depolarized the window in the breakfast room, letting the morning sun stream in through the now transparent sheet of glass. Her attention was caught by something across the street, and she said, in a low voice, "Larry, come here."

Larry Frobisher looked up from his morning coffee. "What is it, hon?"

"The Stanton boys. Come look."

Frobisher sighed. "Who are the Stanton boys, and why should I come look?" But he got up and came over to the window.

"See-over there on the walkway toward the play area," his wife said.

"I see a boy pushing a wheeled contraption and three girls playing with a skip rope," Frobisher said. "Or do you mean that the Stanford boys are dressed up as girls?"

"*Stanton*," she corrected him. "They just moved into the apartment on the first floor."

"Who? The three girls?"

"No, silly! The two Stanton boys and their mother. One of them is in that 'wheeled contraption'. It's called a therapeutic chair."

"Oh? So the poor kid's been hurt. What's so interesting about that, aside from morbid curiosity?"

The boy pushing the chair went around a bend in the walkway, out of sight, and Frobisher went back to his coffee while his wife spoke.

"Their names are Mart and Bart," she said. "They're twins."

"I should think," Frobisher said, applying himself to his breakfast, "that the mother would get a self-powered chair for the boy instead of making the other boy push it."

"The poor boy can't control the chair, dear," said Mrs. Frobisher, still looking out the window after the vanished twins. "There's something wrong with his nervous system. I understand that he was exposed to some kind of radiation when he was only two years old. That's why the chair has to have all those funny instruments built into it. Even his heartbeat has to be controlled electronically."

"Shame," said Frobisher, spearing a bit of sausage. "Kind of rough on both of 'em, I'd guess."

"How do you mean, dear?"

"Well, I mean, like ... well, for instance, why are they going over to the play area? Play games, right? So the one that's well has got to push his brother over there. Can't just get out and go; has to take the brother along, too. Kind of a burden, see?"

Mrs. Frobisher turned away from the window. "Why, Larry! I'm surprised at you. Really! Don't you think the boy *should* take care of his brother?"

"Oh, now, honey, I didn't mean that. It's hard on *both* of 'em. The kid in the chair has to sit there and watch his brother play baseball or jai alai or whatever, while he can't do anything himself. Like I say, kind of rough on both of 'em."

"Well, yes, I suppose it must be. Want some more coffee?"

"Thanks, honey. And another slice of toast, hunh?"

10

Like some horrendous, watchful gargoyle, the Nipe crouched motionlessly on the shadowed roof of the low building. A short projection from the air-conditioning intake was wide enough to keep him from being seen from the air, and the darkness of the roof prevented anyone on the street from seeing the four violet eyes that kept a careful account of all that went on in the store across the way from his observation post.

The lights were still on inside the shop, shedding their glareless brightness through the transparent display windows to fall upon the street outside in large luminous pools. The Nipe knew exactly what each man remaining inside was doing, and approximately what each would be doing for the next few minutes, and he watched with the expectation that his prophecies would be fulfilled.

He had watched long and made a thorough study of this establishment, and tonight he expected to attain the goal for which he had worked so patiently.

This raid was important in two ways. There were pieces of equipment he had to get, and they were in that shop. On the other hand, this raid was, and would be, basically a diversionary tactic. Now that he had located his real target, it was time to create a diversion that would draw his enemy's attention away from his immediate surroundings. This would be a raid that Colonel Walther Mannheim could not ignore!

Two men came out the front door. They spoke to someone still inside. "So long." "See you tomorrow." Then they walked down the street together, conversing in low tones.

The Nipe waited.

Not until a fifth man stopped after he opened the door and flipped a switch on the inside did the Nipe make any motion. Then he flexed his four pairs of limbs in anticipation-but it wasn't quite time to act yet.

The interior lights of the shop went out. Then the man carefully locked the front door, setting the alarms within the shop. Then, serene in the belief that his establishment was thoroughly protected from burglars, he, too, went down the street.

The Nipe waited a few minutes longer before he left his observation post. All was normal, he decided. The time for action had come.

The Nipe moved cautiously along the alley toward the rear of the building that was his target. The night watchman had returned to his cubicle, as he always did after his preliminary inspection of the building's alarm system. He would not leave for some time yet, if he followed his habits. And the Nipe saw no reason why he should not.

Carefully he approached the rear door of the little optical shop.

11

The two massive objects floating in space looked very much like deeply pitted pieces of rock. The larger one, roughly pear-shaped and about a quarter of a mile in its greatest dimension, was actually that —a huge hunk of rock. The smaller —*much* smaller-of the two was not what it appeared to be. It was a phony. Anyone who had been able to conduct a very close personal inspection of it would have recognized it for what it was —a camouflaged spaceboat.

The camouflaged spaceboat was on a near-collision course with reference to the larger mass, although their relative velocities were not great.

At precisely the right time, the smaller drifted by the larger, only a few hundred yards away. The weakness of the gravitational fields generated between the two caused only a slight change of orbit on the part of both bodies. Then they began to separate.

But, during the few seconds of their closest approach, a third body detached itself from the camouflaged spaceboat and shot rapidly across the intervening distance to land on the surface of the floating mountain.

The third body was a man in a spacesuit. As soon as he landed, he sat down, stock-still, and checked the instrument case he held in his hands.

No response. Thus far, then, he had succeeded.

He had had to pick his time precisely. The people who were already on this small planetoid could not use their detection equipment while the planetoid itself was within detection range of Beacon 971, only two hundred and eighty miles away. Not if they wanted to keep from being found. Radar pulses emanating from a presumably lifeless planetoid would be a dead giveaway.

Other than that, they were mathematically safe. Mathematically safe they would be if-and only if-they depended upon the laws of chance. No ship moving through the Asteroid Belt would dare to move at any decent velocity without using radar, so the people on this particular lump of planetary flotsam would be able to spot a ship's approach easily, long before their own weak detection system would register on the pickups of an approaching ship.

The power and range needed by a given detector depends on the relative velocity-the greater that velocity becomes, the more power, the greater range needed. At one mile per second, a ship needs a range of only thirty miles to spot an obstacle thirty seconds away; at ten miles per second, it needs a range of three hundred miles.

The man who called himself Stanley Martin had carefully plotted the orbit of this particular planetoid and had let his spaceboat coast in without using any detection equipment except the visual. It had been necessary, but very risky.

The Asteroid Belt, that magnificently useful collection of stone and metal lumps revolving about the sun between the orbits of Mars and Jupiter, is somewhat like the old-fashioned merry-go-round. If every orbit in the Belt were perfectly circular, the analogy would be more exact. If they were, then every rock in the Belt would follow every other in almost exactly the way every merry-go-round horse follows every other. (The gravitational attraction between the various bodies in the Belt can be neglected. It is much less, on the average, than the gravitational pull between any two horses on a carousel.) If every orbit of those millions upon millions of pieces of rock and metal were precisely circular, then they would constitute the grandest, biggest merry-go-round in the universe.

But those orbits are not circular. And even if they were, they would not remain so long. The great mass of Jupiter would soon pull them out of such perfect orbits and force them to travel about the sun in elliptical paths. And therein lies the trouble.

If their paths were exactly circular, then no two of that vast number of planetoids would ever collide. They would march about the sun in precise order, like the soldiers in a military parade, except that they would retain their spacing much longer than any group of soldiers could possibly manage to do.

But the orbits are elliptical. There is a chance that any two given bodies *might* collide, although the chance is small. The one compensation is that if they do collide they won't strike each other very hard.

The detective was not worried about collision; he was worried about observation. Had the people here seen his boat? If so, had they recognized it in spite of the heavy camouflage? And, even if they only suspected, what would be their reaction?

He waited.

It takes nerve and patience to wait for thirteen solid hours without making any motion other than an occasional flexing of muscles, but he managed that long before the instrument case that he held waggled a meter needle at him. The one tension-relieving factor was the low gravity; the problem of sleeping on a bed of nails is caused by the likelihood of the sleeper accidentally throwing himself off the bed. The probability of puncture or discomfort from the points is almost negligible.

When the needle on the instrument panel flickered, he got to his feet and began moving. He was almost certain that he had not been detected.

Walking was out of the question. This was a silicate-alumina rock, not a nickel-iron one. The group of people that occupied it had deliberately chosen it that way, so that there would be no chance of its being picked out for slicing by one of the mining teams in the Asteroid Belt. Granted, the chance of any given metallic planetoid's being selected was very small-but they had not wanted to take even that chance.

Therefore, without any magnetic field to hold him down, and with only a very tiny gravitic field, the detective had to use different tactics.

It was more like mountain climbing than anything else, except that there was no danger of falling. He crawled over the surface in the same way that an Alpine climber might crawl up the side of a steep slope-seeking handholds and toeholds and using them to propel himself onward. The only difference was that he covered distance a great deal more rapidly than a mountain climber could.

When he reached the spot he wanted, he carefully concealed himself beneath a craggy overhang. It took a little searching to find exactly the right spot, but when he did, he settled himself into place in a small pit and began more elaborate preparations.

Self-hypnosis required nearly ten minutes. The first five or six minutes were taken up in relaxing from his exertions. Gravity notwithstanding, he had had to push his hundred and eighty pounds over a considerable distance. When he was completely relaxed and completely hypnotized, he reached up and cut down the valve that fed oxygen into his suit.

Then-of his own will-he went cataleptic.

A single note, sounded by the instruments in the case at his side, woke him instantly. He came fully awake, as he had commanded himself to do.

Immediately he turned up his oxygen intake, at the same time glancing at the clock dial in his helmet. He smiled. Nineteen days and seven hours. He had calculated it almost precisely.

He wasn't more than an hour off, which was really pretty good, all things considered.

He consulted his instruments again. The supply ship was ten minutes away. The smile stayed on his face as he prepared for further action.

The first two minutes were conscientiously spent in inhaling oxygen. Even under the best cataleptic conditions, the human body tended to slow down too much. He had to get himself prepared for violent movement.

Eight minutes left.

He climbed out of the little grotto where he had concealed himself and moved toward the spot where he knew the airlock to the caverns underneath the planetoid's surface was hidden.

Then again he concealed himself and waited, while he continued to breathe deeply of the highly oxygenated air in his suit. Five minutes before the ship landed, he swallowed eight ounces of the nutrient solution from the tank in the back of his helmet. The solution of amino acids, vitamins, and honey sugar also contained a small amount of stimulant of the dexedrine type and one percent ethanol.

He waited for another minute for the solution to take effect, then he unholstered his gun.

The supply ship wasn't a big one. He had known it wouldn't be. It was only a little larger than the one he had used to come out here. It dropped down to the surface of the small planetoid only ten meters from the hidden trapdoor that led to the airlock beneath the surface.

Suddenly he could hear voices in the earphones of his helmet.

Lasser?

Yeah. It's me, Fritz. I got all the supplies and a nice package of good news.

The airlock trapdoor opened, and a spacesuited figure came out. *How about the deal?*

That's the good news, said the second suited figure as it came from the airlock of the grounded spaceboat. *Another five million.*

The detective, hidden behind the nearby crag of rock, listened and watched for a minute or so while the two men began unloading cases of foodstuffs from the spaceboat. Then, satisfied that it was perfectly safe, he aimed his gun and shot twice in rapid succession.

The range was almost point-blank, and there was, of course, no need to take either gravity or air resistance into account.

The pellets of the shotgun-like charge that blasted out from the gun were small, needle-shaped, and massive. They were oriented point-forward by the magnetic field along the barrel of the weapon. Of the hundreds of charges fired, only a few penetrated the spacesuits of the targets, but those few were enough. The powerful drug in the needle-pointed head of each tiny crystal went directly into the bloodstream of each target.

Each man felt an itching sensation. He had less than two seconds to think about it before unconsciousness overtook him and he slumped nervelessly.

Gun in hand, the detective ran across the intervening space quickly, his body only a few degrees from the horizontal, and his toes paddling rapidly to propel him over the rough rock.

He braked himself to a halt and slapped air patches over the areas where his charges had struck the men's suits, sealing the tiny air leaks, and, at the same time, driving more of the tiny needles into their skins. They would be out for a long time.

Neither of them had yet fallen to the ground. That would take several minutes under this low gravity. He left them to drop and headed toward the open airlock.

This was what he had been waiting for all those nineteen days in cataleptic hypnosis. He couldn't have cut his way into the hideout from the outside; he had had to wait until it was opened, and that time had come only with the supply ship.

Once in the airlock, he touched the control stud that would close the outer door, pump air into the waiting room, and open the inner door. Here was his greatest point of danger-greater, even, than the danger of coming to the planetoid itself, or the danger of waiting nineteen days in a cataleptic trance for the coming of the supply ship. If the ones who remained within suspected anything-anything at all! —then his chances of coming out of this alive were practically nil.

But there was no reason why they should suspect. They should think that the man coming in was one of their own. The radio contact between the men outside had been limited to a few micromilliwatts of power-necessarily, since radio waves of very small wattage can be decoded at tremendous distances in open space. The men inside the planetoid certainly should not have been able to pick up any more than the beginning of the early conversation before it had been cut completely off by the intervening layers of solid rock.

The chamber he entered was a high-speed airlock. Unlike the soundless discharge of his special gun in the outer airlessness, the blast of air that came into the waiting chamber was like a hurricane in noise and force. The room filled with air in a very few seconds.

The detective held on to the handholds tightly while the brief but violent winds buffeted him. He turned as the inner door opened.

His eyes took in the picture in a fraction of a second. In an even smaller fraction, his mind assimilated the picture.

The woman was dark-haired, dark-eyed, and muscular. Her mouth was wide and thick-lipped beneath a large nose.

The man was leaner and lighter, bony-faced, and beady-eyed.

The woman said: "Fritz, what —?"

And then he shot them both with gun number two.

No needle charges this time. Such shots would have blown them both in two, unprotected as they were by spacesuits. The small handgun merely jangled their nerves with a high-powered blast of accurately beamed supersonics. While they were still twitching, he went over and jabbed them with a drug needle.

Then he went on into the hideout.

He had to knock out one more man, whom he found asleep in a small room off the short corridor.

It took a gas bomb to get the two women who were guarding the kid.

He made sure that the BenChaim boy was all right, then he went to the little communications room and called for help.

12

St. Louis hadn't been hit during the Holocaust. It still retained much of the old-fashioned flavor of the nineteenth and twentieth centuries, especially in the residential districts. The old homes, some of them dating clear back to the time of Sam Clemens and the paddle-wheel steamboat, still stood, warm and well preserved.

Bart Stanton liked to walk along those quiet streets of an evening, just to let the placid peacefulness seep into him.

And, knowing it was rather childish, he still enjoyed the small Huckleberry Finn pleasure of playing hooky from the Neurophysical Institute.

Technically, he supposed, he was still a patient there. More, now that he had completely accepted Colonel Walther Mannheim's assignment, he was presumably under military discipline. He assumed that if he had asked permission to leave the Institute's grounds he would have been given that permission without question.

But, like playing hooky or stealing watermelon, it was more fun if it was done on the sly. The boy who comes home feeling deliciously wicked and delightfully sinful after staying away from school all day can have his whole day ruined completely by being told that it was a holiday and the school had been closed. Bart Stanton didn't want to spoil his own fun by asking for permission to leave the grounds when it was so easy for a man with his special abilities to get out without asking.

Besides, there *was* a chance —a small one, he thought-that permission might be refused for one reason or another, and Stanton was fully aware that he would not disobey a direct request-to say nothing of a direct order-that he stay within the walls of the Institute.

He didn't want to run any risk of losing his freedom, small though it was. After five years of mental and physical hell, he felt a need to get out into the world of normal, ordinary, everyday people.

His legs moved smoothly, surely, and unhurriedly, carrying him aimlessly along the resilient walkway, under the warm glow of the streetlights. The people around him walked as casually and with seemingly as little purpose as he did. There was none of the brisk sense of urgency that he felt inside the walls of the Institute.

But he knew he could never get away from that sense of urgency completely, even out here. There were times when it seemed that all he had ever done, all his whole life, was to train himself for the one single purpose of besting the Nipe.

If he wasn't training physically, he was listening to lectures from Dr. George Yoritomo or from Colonel Mannheim. If he wasn't working his muscles, he was laying plans and considering possibilities for the one great goal that seemed to be the focal point of his whole life.

What would happen if he failed?

What would happen if he, the great hyped-up superman, found that the Nipe had only been working at half his normal potential? What would happen if that alien horror simply slashed out with one ultrafast hand and showed Colonel Mannheim and all his watching technicians that they had completely underestimated his alien ability?

What would happen?

Why, Bart Stanton would die, of course, just as hundreds of other human beings had died in the past ten years. Stanton would become another statistic. And then Mannheim's Plan Beta would go into effect. The Nipe would be killed eventually.

But what if he, Stanton, won? Then what?

The people around him were not a part of his world, really. Their thoughts, their motions, their reactions, were slow and clumsy in comparison with his own. Once the Nipe had been conquered, what purpose would there be in the life of Bartholomew Stanton? He was surrounded by people, but he was not one of them. He was immersed in a society that was not his own because it was not, could not be, geared to his abilities and potentials. But there was no other society to turn to, either.

He was not a man "alone, afraid" in a world he had never made. He was a man who had been made for a world, a society, that did not exist.

Women? A wife? A family life?

Where? With whom?

He pushed the thoughts from his mind, the questions unanswered and perhaps unanswerable. In spite of the apparent bleakness of the future, he had no desire to die, and there was, psychologically, the possibility that too much brooding of that kind would evoke a subconscious reaction that could slow him down or cause a wrong decision at a vital moment. A feeling of futility could operate to bring on his death in spite of his conscious determination to win the coming battle with the Nipe.

The Nipe was his first duty. When that job was finished, he would consider the problem of himself. Just because he could not now see the answer to that problem did not mean that no answer existed.

He suddenly realized that he was hungry. He had been walking through Memorial Park, past the museum-an old, worn edifice that was still called the Missouri Pacific Building. There was a small restaurant only a block away.

He reached into his pocket and took out the few coins that were there. Not much, but enough to buy a sandwich and a glass of milk. Because of the trust fund that had been set up when he had started the treatment at the Neurophysical Institute, he was already well off, but he didn't have much cash. What good was cash at the Institute, where everything was provided?

He stopped at a newsvendor, dropped in a coin, and waited for the reproducing mechanism to turn out a fresh paper. Then he took the folded sheets and went on to the restaurant.

He rarely read a newssheet. Mostly, his information about the world that existed outside the walls of the Institute came from the televised newscasts. But, occasionally, he liked to read the small, relatively unimportant little stories about people who had done small, relatively unimportant things-stories that didn't appear in the headlines or the newscasts.

The last important news story that he had heard had come two nights before. The Nipe had robbed an optical products company in Miami. The camera had shown the shop on the screen. Whatever had been used to blow open the vault had been more effective than necessary. It had taken the whole front door of the shop and both windows, too. The bent and twisted paraglass that had lain on the pavement showed how much force had been applied from within.

And yet, the results had not been those of an explosion. It was more as though some tremendous force had *pushed* outward from within. It had not been the shattering shock of high explosive, but some great thrust that had unhurriedly, but irresistibly, moved everything out of its way.

Nothing had been moved very far, as it would have been by a blast. It appeared that everything had simply fallen aside, as though scattered by a giant hand. The main braces of the storefront were still there, bent outward a little, but not broken.

The vault door had been slammed to the floor of the shop, only a few feet from the front door. The vault itself had been farther back, and the camera had showed it standing wide open, gaping. Inside, there had been pieces of fragile glass standing on the shelves, unmoved, unharmed.

The force, whatever it had been, had moved in one direction only, from a point within the vault, just a few feet from the door, pushing outward to tear out the heavy door as though it had been made of paraffin or modeling clay.

Stanton had recognized the vault construction type: the Voisier construction, which, by test, could withstand almost everything known, outside of the actual application of atomic energy itself. In a widely-publicized demonstration several years before, a Voisier vault had been cut open by a team of well-trained, well-equipped technicians. It had taken twenty-one hours for them to breach the wall, and they had had no fear of interruption, or of making a noise, or of setting off the intricate alarms that were built into the safe itself. Not even a borazon drill could make much of an impression on a metal which had been formed under millions of atmospheres of pressure.

And yet the Nipe had taken that door out in a second, without much effort at all.

The crowd that had gathered at the scene of the crime had not been large. The very thought of the Nipe kept people away from places where he was known to have been. The specter of the Nipe evoked a fear, a primitive fear-fear of the dark and fear of the unknown-combined with the rational fear of a very real, very tangible danger.

And yet, there *had* been a crowd of onlookers. In spite of their fear, it is hard to keep human beings from being curious. It was known that the Nipe didn't stay around after he had struck, and, besides, the area was now full of armed men. So the curious came to look and to stare in revulsion at the neat pile of gnawed and bloody bones that had been the night watchman, carefully killed and eaten by the Nipe before he had opened the vault.

Thus curiosity does make fools of us all, and the native hue of caution is crimsoned o'er by the bright red of morbid fascination.

Stanton went through the door of the automatic restaurant and walked over to the vending wall. The big dining room was only about three quarters full of people, and there were plenty of seats available. He fed coins into the proper slots, took his sandwich and milk over to a seat in one corner and made himself comfortable.

He flipped open the newspaper and looked at the front page.

And, for a moment, his brain seemed to freeze.

The story itself was straightforward enough:

BENCHAIM KIDNAPPERS NABBED!

STAN MARTIN DOES IT AGAIN!

CERES, June 3 (*Interplanetary News Service*) —The three men and three women who al-legedly kidnapped 10-year-old Shmuel BenChaim were brought to justice today through the single-handed efforts of Stanley Martin, famed investigator for Lloyd's of London. The boy, held prisoner for more than ten weeks on a small planetoid, was reported in good health.

According to Lt. John Vale of the Planetoid Police, the kidnap gang could not have been taken by direct assault on their hideout because of fear that the boy might be killed.

"The operation required a carefully planned one-man infiltration of their hideout," Lt. Vale said. "Mr. Martin was the man for the job."

Labeled "the most outrageous kidnapping in history", the affair was conceived as a long-term method of gaining control of Heavy Metals Incorporated, controlled by Moishe BenChaim, the boy's father. The details...

But Bart Stanton wasn't interested in the details. After only a glance through the first part of the article, his eyes returned to the picture that had caught his attention. The line of print beneath it identified the picture as being that of a man named Stanley Martin.

But a voice in Bart Stanton's brain said: *Not Stan Martin! The name is Mart Stanton!*

And Bartholomew felt a roar of confusion in his mind-because he didn't know who Mart Stanton was, and because the face in the picture was his own.

13

He was walking again.

He didn't quite remember how he had left the automat, and he really didn't even try to remember.

He was trying to remember other things-further back-before he had...

Before he had *what*?

Before the Institute. Before the beginning of the operations.

The memories were there, all right. He could sense them, floating in some sort of mental limbo, just beyond the grasp of his conscious mind, like the memories of a dream after one has awakened. Each time he would try to reach into the darkness to grasp one of the pieces, it would shatter into smaller bits. The big patterns were too fragile to withstand the direct probing of his conscious mind, and even the resulting fragments did not want to hold still long enough to be analyzed.

And, while a part of his mind probed frantically after the elusive particles of memory, another part of it watched the process with semi-detached amusement.

He had always known there were holes in his memory (*Always? Don't kid yourself, pal!*), but it was disconcerting to find an area that was as full of holes as a used machine-gun target. The whole fabric had been punched to bits.

No man's memory is completely available at any given time. Whatever the recording process is, however completely every bit of data may be recorded during a lifetime, much of it is unavailable. It may be incompletely cross-indexed, or, in some instances, labeled DO NOT SCAN. Or, metaphorically, the file drawer may be locked. It may be that, in many cases, if a given bit of data remains unscanned for a long enough period, it fades into illegibility, never reinforced by the scanning process. Sensory data, coming in from the outside world as it does, is probably permanent. But the thought patterns originating within the mind itself, the processes that correlate and cross-index and speculate on and hypothesize about the sensory data, these are much more fragile. A man might glance once through a Latin primer and have each and every page imprinted indelibly on his recording mechanism and still be unable to make sense out of *Nauta in cubitu cum puella est.*

Sometimes a man is aware of the holes in his memory. ("What *was* the name of that fellow I met at Eddie's party? Can't remember it for the life of me.") At other times, a memory may lay dormant and completely unremembered, leaving no apparent gap, until a tag of some kind brings it up. ("That girl with the long hair reminds me of Suzie Blugerhugle. My gosh! I haven't thought of her in years!") Both factors seemed to be operating in Bart Stanton's mind at this time.

Incredibly, he had never, in the past year at least, had occasion to try to remember much about his past life. He had known who he was without thinking about it particularly, and the rest of his knowledge-language, history, social behavior, politics, geography, and so on-had been readily available for the most part. Ask an educated man to give the product of the primes 2, 13, and 41, or ask him to give the date of the Norman Conquest, and he can give you the answers very quickly. He may have to calculate the first, which will make him pause for a second before answering, but the second will come straight out of his memory records. In neither case does he have to think of where he learned the process or the fact, or who taught it to him, or when he got the information.

But now the picture and the name in the paper had brought forth a reaction in Stanton's mind, and he was trying desperately to bring the information out of oblivion.

Did he have a mother? Surely. But could he remember her? *Yes!* Certainly. A pretty, gentle, rather sad woman. He could remember when she died, although he couldn't remember ever having actually attended the funeral.

What about his father?

Try as he might, he could find no memory whatever of his father, and, at first, that bothered him. He could remember his mother-could almost see her moving around in the apartment where they had lived in ...in ...in Denver! Sure! And he could remember the big building itself, and the block, and even Mrs. Frobisher, who lived upstairs! And the school! And the play area! A great many memories came crowding back, but there was no trace of his father.

And yet...

Oh, of *course*! That was it! His father had been killed in an accident when Martinbart were very young.

Martinbart!

The name flitted through his mind like a scrap of paper in a high wind, but mentally he reached out and grasped it.

Martinbart. Martin-Bart. Mart 'n' Bart. Mart *and* Bart.

The Stanton Twins.

It was very curious, he thought, that he should have forgotten his brother. And even more curious that the name in the paper had not brought him instantly to mind.

Martin, the cripple. Martin, the boy with the poor, weak, radiation-shattered nervous system. The boy who had had to stay in a therapeutic chair all his life because his efferent nerves could not control his body. The boy who couldn't speak. Or, rather, *wouldn't* speak because he was ashamed of the gibberish that resulted.

Martin. The nonentity. The nothing. The nobody.

The one who watched and listened and thought, but could do nothing.

Bart Stanton stopped suddenly and unfolded the newspaper again under the glow of the streetlamp. His memories certainly didn't jibe with *this*!

His eyes ran down the column of type:

Mr. Martin has, in the years since he has been in the Belt, run up an enviable record, both as an insurance investigator and as a police detective, although his connection with the Planetoid Police is, necessarily, an unofficial one. Probably not since Sherlock Holmes has there been such mutual respect and co-operation between the official police and a private investigator.

There was only one explanation, Stanton thought. Martin, too, had been treated by the Institute. His memory was still blurry and incomplete, he knew, but he did suddenly remember that a decision had been made for Martin to take the treatment.

He chuckled a little at the irony of it. It looked as though they hadn't been able to make a superman of Martin, but they *had* been able to make a normal and extraordinarily capable human being of him, he thought. Now it was Bart who was the freak, the odd one.

Turn about is fair play, he thought. But somehow it didn't seem quite fair.

He crumpled the newspaper, dropped it into a nearby waste chute, and walked on through the night toward the Neurophysical Institute.

FOURTH INTERLUDE

"You understand, Mrs. Stanton," said the psychiatrist, "that a great part of Martin's trouble is mental as well as physical. Because of the nature of his ailment, he has withdrawn, pulled himself away from communication with others. If these symptoms had been brought to my attention earlier, the mental disturbance might have been more easily analyzed and treated."

"I suppose so. I'm sorry, Doctor," said Mrs. Stanton. Her manner betrayed weariness and pain. "It was so ... so difficult. Martin could never talk very well, you know, and he just talked less and less as the years went by. It was so slow and so gradual that I never really noticed it."

Poor woman, the doctor thought. *She's not well, herself. She should have married again, years ago, rather than force herself to carry the whole burden alone. Her role as a doting mother hasn't helped either of the boys to overcome the handicaps that were already present.*

"I've honestly tried to do my very best with Martin," Mrs. Stanton went on unhappily. "And so has Bart, I know. When they were younger, Bart used to take him out all the time. They went everywhere together. Of course, I don't expect Bart to do that so much any more. He has his own life to live. He can't take Martin out on dates or things like that. He has interests outside the home now, like other boys his age. That's only normal. But when he's at home, Bart helps me with Martin all the time."

"I understand," said the psychiatrist. *This is no time to tell her that Bartholomew's tests indicate that he has subconsciously resented Martin's presence for a long time*, he thought. *She has enough to worry about.*

"*I* don't understand," said Mrs. Stanton, breaking into sudden tears. "I just don't understand why Martin should behave this way! Why should he just sit there with his eyes closed and ignore everybody? Why should he ignore his mother and his brother? Why?"

The doctor comforted her in a warmly professional manner, then, as her tears subsided, he said, "We don't understand all the factors ourselves, Mrs. Stanton. At first glance, Martin's reactions appear to be those one would expect of schizophrenic withdrawal. But there are certain aspects of the case that make it unusual. His behavior doesn't quite follow the pattern we usually expect from such cases as this. His extreme physical disability has drastically modified the course of his mental development, and, at the same time, made it difficult for us to make any analysis of his mental state." *If only*, he added to himself, *she had followed the advice of her family physician, years ago. If she had only put the boy under the proper care, none of this would have happened.*

"Is there *anything* we can do, Doctor?" she asked.

"We don't know yet," he said gently. He considered for a moment, then said: "Mrs. Stanton, I'd like for you to leave both of the boys here for a few days, so that we can perform further tests. That will help us a great deal in evaluating the circumstances, and help us get at the root of Martin's trouble."

She looked at him with a little surprise. "Why, yes, of course-if you think it's necessary. But ... why should Bart stay?"

The doctor weighed his words carefully before he spoke.

"Bart will be what we call a 'control', Mrs. Stanton. Since the boys are genetically identical, they should have been a great deal alike, in personality as well as in body, if it hadn't been for Martin's accident. In other words, our tests of Bart will tell us what Martin *should* be like. That way, we can tell just how much and in what way Martin deviates from what he should ideally be. Do you understand?"

"Yes. Yes, I see. All right, Doctor-whatever you say."

After Mrs. Stanton had left, the psychiatrist sat quietly in his chair and stared thoughtfully at his desk top for several minutes. Then, making his decision, he picked up a small book that lay on his desk and looked up a number in Arlington, Virginia. He punched out the number on his phone, and when the face appeared on his screen he said, "Hello, Sidney. Busy right now?"

"Not particularly. Not for a few minutes. What's up?"

"I have a very interesting case out here that I'd like to talk to you about. Do you happen to have a telepath who's strong enough to take a meshing with an insane mind? If my suspicions are correct, I will need a man with an absolutely impregnable sense of identity, because he's going to get into the weirdest situation I've ever come across."

14

The Nipe squatted, brooding, in his underground nest, waiting for the special crystallization process to take place in the sodium-gold alloy that was forming in the reactor.

How long? he wondered. He was not thinking of the complex crystallization reaction; he knew the timing of that to a fraction of a second. His dark thoughts were, instead, focused inwardly, upon himself.

How long would it be before he would be able to construct the communicator that would span the light-years of intervening distance and put him in touch with his own race again? How long would it be before he could again hold discourse with reasonable beings? How much longer would he have to be stranded on this planet, surrounded by an insane society composed of degraded, insane beings?

The work was going incredibly slowly. He had known at the beginning that his knowledge of the basic arts required to build a communicator was incomplete, but he had not realized just how painfully inadequate it was. Time after time, his instruments had simply refused to function because of some basic flaw in their manufacture-some flaw that an expert in that field could have pointed out at once. Time after time, equipment had had to be rebuilt almost from the beginning. And, time after time, only cut-and-try methods were available for correcting his errors.

Not even his prodigious and accurate memory could hold all the information that was necessary for the work, and there were no reference tapes available, of course. They had all been destroyed when his ship had crashed.

He had long since given up any attempt to understand the functioning of the mad pseudo-civilization that surrounded him. He was quite certain that the beings he had seen could not possibly be the real rulers of this society, but he had no inkling, as yet, as to who the real rulers were.

As to *where* they were, that question seemed a little easier to answer. It was highly probable that they were out in space, on the asteroids that his instruments had detected when he was dropping in toward this planet so many years before. He had made an error then in not landing in the Belt, but at no time since had he experienced the emotion of regret or wished he had done differently; both thoughts would have been incomprehensible to the Nipe. He had made an error; the circumstances had been checked and noted; he would not make that error again.

What further action could be taken by a logical mind?

None. The past was immutable and unchangeable. It existed only as a memory in his own mind, and there was no way to change that indelible record, even had the Nipe wished to do so insane a thing.

Surely, he thought, the real rulers must know of his existence. He had tried, by his every action, to show that he was a reasoning, intelligent, and civilized being. Why, then, had they taken no action?

There was, of course, the possibility that the rulers cared very little for their subjects here on Earth, that they ignored what went on most of the time. Still, it would seem that they would recognize the actions of one of their own kind and take steps to investigate.

He was still not absolutely certain about Colonel Walther Mannheim. Was he a Real Person or merely an underling? The information on the man was pitifully small. It would, of course, be possible to wait, to see how Colonel Walther Mannheim behaved if and when he discovered the Nipe's nest. But if he had not discovered it after all these years-and the information indicated that he had been looking almost since the first-then it was unlikely that he was a Real Person. In which case, it would be dangerous to allow him to find the nest.

No, the best plan of action would be to go to Colonel Walther Mannheim first.

15

Pok! Pok! Ping!
  Pok! Pok! Ping!
  Pok! Pok! Ping!
  Pok! Pok! Ping!

The action around the handball court was beautiful to watch. The robot mechanism behind Bart Stanton would fire out a ball at random intervals ranging from a tenth to a quarter of a second, bouncing them off the wall in a random pattern. Stanton would retrieve the ball before it hit the ground and bounce it off the wall again to strike the target on the moving robot. Stanton had to work against a machine; no ordinary human being could have given him any competition.

  Pok! Pok! Ping!
  Pok! Pok! Ping!
  Pok! Pok! PLUNK.

"One miss," Stanton said to himself. But he fielded the next one nicely and slammed it home.

  Pok! Pok! Ping!

The physical therapist who was standing to one side, well out of the way of those hard-slammed, fast-moving drives, glanced at his watch. It was almost time.

  Pok! Pok! Ping!

The machine, having delivered its last ball, shut itself off with a smug click. Stanton turned away from the handball court and walked toward the physical therapist, who was holding out a robe for him.

"That was good, Bart," he said. "Real good."

"One miss," Stanton said as he shrugged into the robe.

"Yeah. Your timing was off a shade there, I guess. It's hard for me to tell till I look at the slow-motion photographs. Your arms and hands are just blurs to me when they're moving that fast. But you managed to chop another ten seconds off your previous record, anyway."

Stanton looked at him. "You reset the timer again," he said accusingly. But there was a grin on his face.

The P.T. man grinned back. "Yup. Come on, step into the mummy case." He waved toward the narrow niche in the wall of the court, a niche just big enough to hold a standing man. Stanton stepped in, and various instrument pickups came out of the walls and touched him at various points on his body. Hidden machines recorded his heartbeat, his blood pressure, his brain activity, his muscular tension, his breathing, and several other factors.

After a minute the P.T. man said, "Okay, Bart, that's it. Let's hit the steam box."

Stanton stepped out of the niche and accompanied the therapist to another room, where he took off the robe again and sat down on the small stool inside an ordinary steam box. The box closed, leaving his head free, and the box began to fill with steam.

"Did I ever tell you just what it is that I don't like about that machine?" Stanton asked as the therapist draped a heavy towel around his head.

"Nope. Didn't know you had any gripe. What is it?"

"You can't gloat after you beat it. You can't walk over and pat it on the shoulder and say, 'Well, better luck next time, old man.' It isn't a good loser, and it isn't a bad loser. The damned thing doesn't even know it lost, and even if it did, it wouldn't care."

"Yeah, I see what you mean," said the P.T. man, chuckling. "You beat the pants off it and what d'you get? Nothing. Not even a case of the sulks out of it."

"Exactly. And what's worse, I know perfectly good and well that it's only half trying. The stupid gadget could beat me easily if you just turned that knob over a little more."

"Yeah, sure. But you're not competing against the machine, anyway," the therapist said. "What you're doing, you're competing against yourself, trying to beat your own record."

"I know. And what happens when I can't do *that* any more, either?" Stanton asked. "I can't just go on getting better and better forever. I've got limits, you know."

"Sure," said the therapist easily. "So does anybody. So does a golf player, for instance. You take a golf player, he goes out and practices by himself to try to beat his own record."

"Bunk! Hogwash! The real fun in *any* game is beating someone else! The big kick in golf is winning over the other guy in a twosome."

"How about crossword puzzles or solitaire?"

"When you solve a crossword puzzle, you've beaten the guy who made up the puzzle. When you play solitaire, you're playing against the laws of chance, and that can become pretty boring unless there's money on it. And, in that case, you're actually trying to beat the guy who's betting against you. What I'd like to do is get out on the golf course with someone else and do my best and then lose. Honestly."

"With a handicap ..." the therapist began. Then he grinned weakly and stopped. On the golf course, Stanton was impossibly good. It had taken him a little while to get the knack of it, but as soon as he got control of his club and knew the reactions of the ball, his score started plummeting. Now it was so low as to be almost ridiculous. One long drive to the green and one putt to the cup. An easy thirty-six strokes for eighteen holes! An occasional hole-in-one sometimes brought his score down below that; an occasional wormcast or stray wind sometimes brought it up.

"Sure," said Stanton. "A handicap. What kind of a handicap do you want me to give you to induce you to make a fifty-dollar bet on a handball game with me?"

The physical therapist could imagine himself trying to get under one of Stanton's lightning-like returns. The thought of what would happen to his hand if he were accidentally to catch one made him wince.

"We wouldn't even be playing the same game," said Stanton.

The therapist stepped back and looked at Stanton. "You know," he said puzzledly, "you sound bitter."

"Sure I'm bitter," Stanton said. "All I ever get is just exercise. All the fun has gone out of it." He sighed and grinned. There was no point in upsetting the P.T. man. "I guess I'll just have to stick to cards and chess if I want competition. Speed and strength don't help anything if I'm holding two pair against three of a kind."

Before the therapist could say anything, the door opened and a tall, lean man stepped into the foggy air of the room. "You are broiling a lobster?" he asked the P.T. man blandly.

"Steaming a clam," the therapist corrected. "When he's done, I'll pound him to chowder."

"Excellent. I came for a clambake."

"You're early, then, George," Stanton said. He didn't feel much in the mood for lightness, and the appearance of Dr. Yoritomo did nothing to improve his humor.

George Yoritomo beamed broadly, crinkling up his narrow, heavy-lidded eyes. "Ah! A talking clam! Excellent! How much longer does this fine specimen of clamhood have to cook?" he asked the P.T. man.

"About twenty-three more minutes."

"Excellent!" said Dr. Yoritomo. "Would you be so good as to return at the end of that time?"

The therapist opened his mouth, closed it, then opened it again, and said: "Sure, Doc. I can get some other stuff done. I'll see you in twenty-three minutes. But don't let him out of there till I get back." He went out through the far door.

After the door closed, Dr. Yoritomo pulled up a chair and sat down. "There have been new developments," he said, "as you may have surmised."

The physical therapist, like many other of the personnel around the Institute, knew of Stanton's abilities, but he didn't know the purpose of the long series of operations that had made him what he was. Such persons knew about Stanton himself, but they knew nothing of any connection with the Nipe, although they might suspect. And all of them kept their knowledge and their suspicions to themselves.

"I guessed," Stanton said. "What is it, George?" He flexed his muscles under the caress of the hot, moist currents in the box.

He wondered why it was so important that the psychologist interrupt him while he was relaxing after strenuous exercise. Yoritomo looked excited in spite of his attempt to be calm. And yet Stanton knew that, whatever it was, it wasn't anything tremendously urgent or Dr. Yoritomo would be acting a great deal differently.

Yoritomo leaned forward in his chair, his thin lips in an excited smile, his black-irised eyes sparkling. "I had to come tell you. The sheer, utter beauty of it is too much to contain. Three times in a row was almost absolute, Bart. The probability that our hypotheses were correct was computed as straight nines to seven decimals. But now! The fourth time! Straight nines to *twelve* decimals!"

Stanton lifted an eyebrow. "Your Oriental calm is deserting you, George. I'm not reading you."

Yoritomo's smile became broader. "Ah! Sorry. I refer to the theory we have been discussing. About the peculiar mentality of our friend, the Nipe. You remember?"

Stanton remembered. After six years of watching the recorded actions of the Nipe, Dr. Yoritomo had evolved a theory about the kind of mentality that lay behind the four baleful violet eyes in that snouted alien head. In order that his theory be validated, it was necessary that the theory be able to predict, in broad terms, the future actions of the Nipe. Evidently that proof had now come. The psychologist was smiling and rubbing his long, bony hands together. For Dr. George Yoritomo, that was almost the equivalent of hysterical excitement.

"We have been able to predict the behavior of the Nipe!" he said. "For the fourth time in succession!"

"Great," Stanton said. "Congratulations, George. But how does that fit in with the rule you once told me about? You know, the one about experimental animals."

"Ah, yes," Yoritomo said, nodding his head agreeably. "The Harvard Law of Animal Behavior. 'A genetically standardized strain, under precisely controlled laboratory conditions, when subjected to carefully calibrated stimuli, will behave as it damned well pleases.' Yes. Very true."

He held up a cautionary finger. "But an animal could not do otherwise, could it? Only as it pleases. Could it do anything else? It could not please to behave as something it is not, could it?"

"Draw me a picture," Stanton said.

"What I mean," Yoritomo said, "is that any organism is limited in its choice of behavior. A hamster, for example, cannot choose to behave in the manner of a rhesus monkey. A dog cannot choose to react as a mouse would react. If I prick a white mouse with a needle, it may squeal or bite or jump-but it will not bark. Never. Nor will it, under any circumstances, leap to a trapeze, hang by its tail, and chatter curses at me. Never."

Stanton chuckled, but he didn't comment.

"By observing an organism's reactions," the psychologist continued, "one can begin to see a pattern. After long enough observation, the pattern almost approaches certainty. If, for instance, I tell you that I put an armful of hay into a certain animal's enclosure, and that the animal trotted over, ate the hay, and brayed, then you will be able to tell me with reasonable certainty whether or not the animal had long ears. Do you see?"

"Sure. But you haven't been able to pinpoint the Nipe's activities that easily yet, have you?" Stanton asked.

"Ah, no," said Yoritomo. "Not at all. That was merely an analogy, and we must not make the mistake of carrying an analogy too far. The more intelligent a creature is, the greater, in general, is its scope of action. The Nipe is far from being so simple as a monkey or a hamster. On the other hand —" He smiled widely, showing bright, white teeth. " —he is not so bright as a human being."

"What?" Stanton looked at him skeptically. "I wouldn't say he was exactly stupid, George. What about all those prize gadgets of his?" He blinked. "Wipe the sweat off my forehead, will you? It's running into my eyes."

Dr. Yoritomo wiped with the towel as he continued. "Ah, yes. He is quite capable in that respect, my friend. Quite capable. That is because of his great memory-at once his finest asset and his greatest curse."

He draped the towel around Stanton's head again and stepped back, his face unsmiling. "Imagine having a near-perfect memory, Bart."

Stanton's jaw muscles tightened a little before he spoke. "I think I'd like it," he said.

Yoritomo shrugged slightly. "Perhaps you would. But it would most certainly not be the asset you think. Look at it very soberly, my friend.

"The most difficult teaching job in the world is the attempt to teach an organism something that that organism already knows. True? Yes. If a man already knows the shape of the Earth, it will do you no good to teach him. If he *knows*, for example, that the Earth is flat, but round like a pancake, your contention that it is round like a ball will make no impression upon his mind whatever. He *knows*, you see. He *knows*.

"Now. Imagine a race with a perfect memory —a memory that never fades. A memory in which each bit of data is as bright and as fresh as the moment it was imprinted, and as readily available as the data stored in a robot's mind. It is, in effect, a robotic memory.

"If you put false data into the memory banks of a mathematical computer-such as telling it that the square of two is five-you cannot correct that error simply by telling it the true fact that the square of two is four. No. First you must remove the erroneous data. Not so?"

"Agreed," Stanton said.

"Very good. Then let us look at the Nipe race, wherever it was spawned in this universe. Let us look at the race a long time back-way back when they first became *Nipe sapiens*. Back when they first developed a true language. Each little Nipe child, as it is born or hatched or budded-whatever it is they do-is taught as rapidly as possible all the things it must know in order to survive. And once a little Nipelet is taught a thing, it *knows*. That knowledge is there, and it is permanent, and it can be brought instantly to the fore. And if it is taught a falsehood, then it cannot be taught the truth. You see?"

Stanton thought about it. "Well, yes. But eventually there are going to be cases where reality doesn't jibe with what he's been taught, aren't there? And wouldn't cold reality force a change?"

"Ah. In some cases, yes. In most, no," said Yoritomo. "Look: Suppose one of these primordial Nipes runs across a tiger-or whatever large carnivore passes for a tiger on their home planet. This Nipe, let us say, has never seen a tiger before, so he does not observe that this particular tiger is old, ill, and weak. It is, as a matter of fact, on its last legs. Our primordial Nipe hits it on the head, and it drops dead. He drags the body home for the family to feed upon.

"How did you kill it, Papa?'

"'Why, it was the simplest thing in the world, my child. I walked up to it, bashed it firmly on the noggin, and it died. That is the way to kill tigers.'"

Yoritomo smiled. "It is also a good way to kill Nipes. Eh?" He took the towel and wiped Stanton's brow again.

"The error," he continued, "was made when Papa Nipe made the generalization from *one* tiger to *all* tigers. If tigers were rare, this erroneous bit of lore might be passed on for many generations unchecked and spread through the Nipe community as time passed. Those who did learn that most tigers are *not* conquered by walking up to them and hitting them on the noggin undoubtedly died before they could pass this new bit of information on. Then, perhaps, one day a Nipe survived the ordeal. His mind now contained conflicting information which must be resolved. He *knows* that tigers are killed in this way. He also *knows* that this one was not so obliging as to die. What is wrong? Ha! He has the solution! Plainly, *this* particular beast *was not a tiger!*"

"How does he explain that to the others?" Stanton asked.

"What does he tell his children?" Yoritomo asked rhetorically. "Why, first he tells them how tigers are killed. You walk up to one and bash it on the head. But then he warns his little Nipelets that there is an animal around that looks *just like* a tiger, but it is *not* a tiger. One should not make the mistake of thinking it *is* a tiger or one will get oneself badly hurt. Now, since the only way to tell the true tiger from the false is to give it a hit on the head, and since that test may prove rather injurious, if not absolutely fatal, to the Nipe who tries it, it follows that one is better off if one scrupulously avoids all animals that look like tigers. You see?"

"Yeah," said Stanton. "Some snarks are boojums."

"Exactly! Thank you for that allusion," Yoritomo said with a smile. "I must remember to use it in my report."

"It seems to me to follow," Stanton said musingly, "that there would inevitably be some things that they'd never learn the truth about, once they had gotten the wrong idea into their heads."

"Ah! Indeed. Absolutely true. It is precisely that which led me to formulate my theory in the first place. How else are we to explain that the Nipe, for all his tremendous technical knowledge, is nonetheless a member of a society that is still in the ancient ritual-taboo stage of development?"

"A savage?"

Yoritomo laughed softly. "As to his savagery, I think no one on Earth would disagree. But they are not the same thing. What I do mean is that the Nipe is undoubtedly the most superstitious and bigoted being on the face of this planet."

There was a knock on the door of the steam room.

"Yes?" said Dr. Yoritomo.

The physical therapist stuck his head in. "Sorry to interrupt, but the clam is done. I'll have to give him a rubdown, Doc."

"Perfectly all right," Yoritomo said. "We had almost finished. Think over what I have said, eh, Bart?"

"Yeah, sure, George," Stanton said abstractedly. Yoritomo left, and Stanton got up on the rubdown table and lay prone. The therapist, seeing that his patient was in no mood for conversation, proceeded with the massage in silence.

Stanton lay on the table, his head pillowed in his arms, while the therapist rubbed and kneaded his muscles. The pleasant sensation formed a background for his thoughts. For the first time, Stanton was seeing the Nipe as an individual-as a person-as a thinking, feeling being.

We have a great deal in common, you and I, he thought. *Except that you're a lot worse off than I am.*

I'm actually feeling sorry for the poor guy, Stanton thought. *Which, I suppose, is a hell of a lot better than feeling sorry for myself. The only real, basic difference between us freaks is that you're more of a freak than I am. "Molly O'Grady and the Colonel's lady are sisters under the skin."*

Where'd that come from? Something I learned in school, no doubt-like the snarks and the boojums.

He would answer to Hi! *or to any loud cry,*

Such as Fry me! *or* Fritter my wig!

Who was that? The snark? No. The snark had a flavor like that of will-o'-the-wisp. And I must remember to distinguish those that have feathers, and bite, from those that have whiskers, and scratch.

Damn *this memory of mine!*

Or can I even call it mine when I can't even use it?

"For now we see through a glass, darkly; but then face to face: now I know in part; but then shall I know even as also I am known."

Another jack-in-the-box thought popping up from nowhere.

The only way I'll ever get all of this stuff straightened out in my mind is to get more information. And it doesn't look as though anyone is going to give it to me on a platter, either. The Institute men seem to be awfully chary about giving information away, even to me. George even had to chase away old rub-and-pound (That feels good!) before he would talk about the Nipe. Can't blame 'em for that, of course. There'd be hell to pay for everyone around if the general public ever found out that the Nipe has been kept as a pet for six years.

How many people has he killed in that time? Twenty? Thirty? How much blood does Colonel Mannheim have on his hands?

Though they know not why,

Or for what they give,

Still, the few must die,

That the many may live.

I wonder whether I read all that stuff complete or just browsed through a copy of Bartlett's Quotations.
Fragments.

We've got to get organized around here, brother. Colonel Mannheim's puppet is going to have to cut his strings and do a Pinocchio.

16

Colonel Walther Mannheim unlocked the door of his small suite of rooms in the Officers' Barracks. God! he was tired. It wasn't so much physical exhaustion as mental and emotional release from the tension he had been under for the preceding few hours. Or had it been years?

He dropped his heavy briefcase on a nearby chair, took off his cap and dropped it on the briefcase.

He stood there for a moment, looking tiredly around. Everything was in order, as usual. He seldom came to Government City any more. Twenty or so visits in the last ten years, and only a dozen of them had been long enough to force him to spend the night in his old suite at the World Police Headquarters at the southern end of the island. He didn't like to stay in Government City; it made him uneasy, being this close to the Nipe's underground nest. The Nipe had too many taps into government communication channels, too many ways of seeing and hearing what went on here in the nerve center of civilization.

One of the most difficult parts of this whole operation had been the careful balancing of information flow through those channels that the Nipe had tapped. To stop using them would betray immediately to that alien mind that his taps had been detected. The information flow must go on as usual. There was no way to censor the information, either, although it was known that the Nipe relied on them for planning his raids. But since there was no way of knowing, even after years of observation, what sort of thing the Nipe would be wanting next, there was no way of knowing which information should be removed from the tapped channels.

And, most certainly, removing *all* information about every possible material that the Nipe might want would make him even more suspicious than simply shutting down the channels altogether. To shut them down would only indicate that the human government had detected his taps; to censor them heavily would indicate that a trap was being laid.

It was even impossible to censor out news about the Nipe. That, too, would have invited suspicion. So a special corps of men had been set up, a group whose sole job was to investigate every raid of the Nipe. Every raid produced a flurry of activity by this special group. They rushed out to look over the scene of the raid, prowled around, and did everything that might be expected of an investigative body. Their reports were sent in over the usual channels. All the actual data they came up with was sent straight through the normal channels-but the conclusions they reached from that data were not. Always, in spite of everything, the messages indicated that the police were as baffled as before.

All other information relating to the Nipe went through special channels known to be untapped by the Nipe.

And yet, there was no way to be absolutely certain of the sum total of the information that the Nipe received. Believing, as he did, in the existence of Real People, he would necessarily assume that *their* communication systems were hidden from him, and the more difficult they were to find, the more certain he would be that they existed. And it was impossible to know what information the Nipe picked up when he was out on a raid, away from the spying devices that had been hidden in his tunnels.

Mannheim walked across the small living room to the sideboard that stood against one wall and opened a door. Fresh ice, soda, and a bottle of Scotch were waiting for him. He took one of the ten-ounce glasses, dropped in three of the hard-frozen cubes of ice, added a precisely measured ounce and a half of Scotch, and filled the glass to within an inch of the brim with soda. Holding the glass in one hand, he walked around the little apartment, checking everything with a sort of automatic abstractedness. The air conditioner was pouring sweet, cool, fresh air into the room; the windows-heavy, thick slabs of paraglass welded directly into the wall-admitted the light from the courtyard outside, but admitted nothing else. There was no need for them to open, because of the air conditioning. A century before, some buildings still had fire escapes running down their outsides, but modern fireproofing had rendered such anachronisms unnecessary.

But his mind was only partly on his surroundings. He went into the bedroom, sat down on the edge of the bed, took a long drink from the cold glass in his hand, and then put it on the nightstand. Absently he began pulling off his boots. His thoughts were on the Executive Session he had attended that afternoon.

"How much longer, do you think, Colonel?"

"A few weeks, sir. Perhaps less."

"There was another raid in Miami, Colonel. Another man died. We could have prevented that death, Colonel. We could have prevented a great many deaths in the past six years."

And what answer was there to that? The Executive Council knew that the deaths were preventable in only one way-by killing the Nipe. And they had long ago agreed that the knowledge in that alien mind was worth the sacrifice. But, as he had known would happen when they made the decision six years before, there were some of them who had, inevitably, weakened. Not all-not even a majority-but a minority that was becoming stronger.

It had been, to a great degree, Mannheim's arguments that had convinced them then, and now they were tending to shift the blame for their decision to Mannheim's shoulders.

Most of the Executives were tough-minded, realistic men. They were not going to step out now unless there were good reason for it. But if the subtle undercutting of the vacillating minority weakened Mannheim's own resolve, or if he failed to give solid, well-reasoned answers to their questions, then the whole project would begin to crumble rapidly.

He had not directly answered the Executive who had pointed out that many lives could have been saved if the Nipe had been killed six years ago. There was no use in fighting back on such puerile terms.

"Gentlemen, within a few weeks, we will be ready to send Stanton in after the Nipe. If that fails, we can blast him out of his stronghold within minutes afterwards. But if we stop now, if we allow our judgment to be colored at this point, then all those who have died in the past six years will have died in vain."

He had gone on, exploring and explaining the ramifications of the plans for the next few weeks, but he had carefully kept it on the same level. It had been an emotional sort of speech, but it had been purposely so, in answer to the sort of emotionalism that the weakening minority had attempted to use on him.

Men had died, yes. But what of that? Men had died before for far less worthwhile causes. And men, do what they will, will die eventually. In the back of his mind, he had recalled the battle-cry of some sergeant of the old United States Marines during an early twentieth-century war. As he led his men over the top, he had shouted, *"Come on, you sons of bitches! Do you wanna live forever?"*

But Mannheim hadn't mentioned it aloud to the Executive Council.

Nor had he pointed out that ten thousand times as many people had died during the same period through preventable accidents. That would not have had the effect he wanted.

These particular men had died for this particular purpose. They had not asked to die. They had not known they were being sacrificed. None of them could be said to have died a hero's death. They had died simply because they were in a particular place at a particular time.

They had been allowed to die for a specific purpose. To abort that purpose at this time would be to make their deaths, retroactively, murder.

Mannheim put his head on the pillow and lifted his feet up on the bed. All he wanted was a few minutes of relaxation. He'd get ready for sleep later. He pressed the control button on the bedframe that lifted the head of the bed up so that he was in a semi-reclining position. He picked up his drink and took a second long pull from it.

Then he touched the phone switch and put the receiver to his ear.

"Beta-beta," he said when he heard the tone.

He heard the hum, and he knew that the ultraprivate phone on the desk of Dr. Farnsworth, in St. Louis, was signaling. Then Farnsworth's voice came over the linkage.

"F here."

"*M* here," Mannheim replied. Then he asked guardedly, "Any sign of our boy?"

"None."

"Keep on him," Mannheim said. "Let me know immediately."

"Will do. Any further?"

"No. Carry on." Mannheim cut off the phone.

Where the hell had Stanton disappeared to, and why? He had wanted to bring the young man to Government City to show him off before the Executives. It would have helped. But Stanton had disappeared.

Mannheim was well aware that Stanton had been in the habit of leaving the Institute for long walks during the evenings, but this was the first time he had been gone for twenty-four hours. And even Yoritomo, that master psychologist, had been unable to give any solid reason for Stanton's disappearance.

"You must remember, my dear Colonel," Yoritomo had said, "our young Mr. Stanton is a great deal more complex in his thinking than is our friend the Nipe."

A hell of a job for a police officer, Mannheim thought to himself. *I know where the criminal is, but I have to hunt for the only cop on Earth who can arrest him.*

He drained his glass, put it on the nightstand, and closed his eyes to think.

An operator on duty at the spy screens that watched every move of the Nipe while he was in the tunnels underneath Government City thumbed down a switch and said, "All stations alert. Subject is moving southward toward exit, carrying raiding equipment."

It was all that was necessary. The Nipe could not be followed after he left his lair, but the proper groups would be standing by. Somewhere, the Nipe would hit and raid again. Somewhere, there were human lives in danger.

All anyone could do was wait.

Cautiously and carefully, the Nipe lifted his head out of the cool salt water of the Hudson River, near the point where it widened into New York Harbor-still so called after the city that had been the greatest on the North American continent before the violence of a sun bomb had demolished it forever.

He looked around carefully to get his bearings, then submerged again. The opening into the ancient sewer was nearby. Once into that network, he would know exactly where he was heading. It had taken weeks to find his way around within the unexplored maze of the old sewers, and he had been uncertain whether they would lead him to the place he intended to visit, but luck had been with him.

Now he knew exactly where he wanted to go, and exactly what he would find there.

He had avoided Government City itself since his first appearance there, shortly after his arrival, just as he had, as much as possible, avoided ever striking in the same place more than once. But now that it had become necessary, he went about his work with the same cool determination that had always marked his activities.

He knew his destination, too. He knew the two rooms thoroughly, having explored them carefully and gone away undetected. And now that he knew the one he sought was in those rooms, he was ready to make his final investigation of the man.

He swam on through the utter blackness of the brackish water until his head broke surface again. Then he went on along the great conduits that were above the level of the sea.

Captain Davidson Greer sat in the gun tower that overlooked the Officers' Barracks and the courtyard surrounding the five-story building. He was a tall, solidly built man in his early thirties, with dark gray-green eyes and dark blond hair. He didn't particularly care for gun-tower duty, but this sort of thing couldn't be left to anyone who was not in on the secret of the Nipe. As long as Colonel Mannheim was here in Government City, there would be special officers guarding him instead of the usual guard contingent.

Not that Captain Greer was actually expecting the Nipe to make any attempt on the colonel's life; that was too remote to be worried about. But the gun towers had been erected fifty or more years before because there were always those who wanted to attempt assassination. Officers of the World Police had not enjoyed great popularity during the reconstruction period after the Holocaust. The petty potentates who had set themselves up as autocratic rulers in various spots over the Earth had quite often decided that the best way to get the WP off their backs was to kill someone, and quite often that someone was a Police officer. Disgruntled nationalists and fanatics of all kinds had tried at various times to kill one officer or another. The protection was needed then.

Even now there were occasional assassins who attempted to invade World Police Headquarters, but they were usually stopped long before they got into the enclosure itself.

Still, there was always the chance. There had been, in the past few years, an undercurrent of rebellion all over Earth because of the Nipe. The monster hadn't been killed, and there were those who screamed that the failure was due to the inefficiency of the Police.

One attempt had already been made on the life of a Major Thorensen because he had failed to get the Nipe after a raid in Leopoldville. The would-be assassin had been cut down just before he threw a grenade that would have killed half a dozen men. Captain Greer had been assigned to make sure that no such attempt would succeed with Colonel Mannheim.

He could see the length of the hallway that led to Colonel Mannheim's suite. The hallway had been purposely designed for watching from the gun tower. To one who was inside, it looked like an ordinary hallway, stretching down the length of the building. But it was walled with a special plastic that, while opaque to visible light, was perfectly transparent to infra-red. To the ordinary unaided eye, the walls of the building presented a blank face to the gun tower, but to the eye of an infra-red scope, the hallways of all five floors looked as though they were long, glass-enclosed terraces. And those walls were neither the ferro-concrete of the main building nor the pressure glass of the windows, but ordinary heavy-gauge plastic. To the bullets that could be spewed forth from the muzzle of the heavy-caliber, high-powered machine gun in the tower, those walls were practically nonexistent.

Captain Greer surveyed the hallways with his infra-red binoculars. Nothing. The halls were empty. He lowered the binoculars and lit a cigarette. Then he put his eyes to the aiming scope of the gun and swiveled the muzzle a little. The aiming scope showed nothing either.

He leaned back and exhaled a cloud of smoke.

Colonel Mannheim blinked and looked at the ceiling. It took him a minute to re-orient himself. Then he grinned rather sheepishly, realizing that he had dozed off with his clothes on. Even worse, the pressure at his hip told him that he hadn't even bothered to take his sidearm off. He sat up and swung his feet to the floor, then glanced at his wrist. Three in the morning.

And the moral of that, my dear Walther, he told himself, *is that a tired man should put on his pajamas first, before he lies down and drinks a Scotch.*

He stood up. Might as well put his pajamas on and get to bed. He would have to be back in St. Louis by ten in the morning, so he ought to get as much sleep as possible.

The phone chimed.

He scooped it up and became instantly awake as he heard the voice of Captain Greer from the gun tower that faced the outer wall. "Colonel, the Nipe is just outside the wall of your apartment, in the hallway. I have him in my sights." He was trying to stay calm, Mannheim could tell by his voice, but he rattled the words off with machine-gun rapidity.

Mannheim thought rapidly. Whatever the Nipe was up to, it wouldn't include planting a bomb or anything that might kill anyone accidentally. If there was a life in danger, it was his own, and the danger would come from the Nipe's hands, not from any device or weapon.

He was thankful that it was Captain Greer up in that tower, not an ordinary guard who would have fired the instant he saw the alien through the infra-red-transparent walls. Even so, he knew that the captain's fingers must be tightening on those triggers. No human being could do otherwise with that monster in his sights.

Mannheim spoke very calmly and deliberately. "Captain, listen very carefully. Do *not* —I repeat, do *not*, under any circumstances whatever, fire that gun. Understand?"

"Yes, sir."

"What's he doing?"

"I can't tell, sir. He has some sort of gadget in his hands, but he just seems to be squatting there."

"At the door?"

"No. To the left of it, at the wall."

"You have your cameras going?"

"Yes, sir."

"All right. Get everything that happens. Under no circumstances shoot or give the alarm — *even if he kills me.* Let him go. I don't think that will happen, but if it does, let him go. I think I can talk to him. I don't think there's much danger. I'm going to leave the phone open so you can record everything, and —"

There was a muffled noise from the living room. He heard Captain Greer's gasp as he turned. He could see through the bedroom door to the wall of the living room. A large section of the ferro-concrete wall had sagged away and collapsed, having suddenly lost its tensile strength. On the top of the rubble, frozen for a long instant, stood the Nipe, watching with those four glowing violet eyes.

Mannheim let go the phone and turned to face the monster, and in that instant he realized his mistake.

The Nipe stared at the human being. Was this, at last, a Real Person? It was surprising that the man should be awake. Only a minute before, the instruments had shown him to be in the odd cataleptic state that these creatures lapsed into periodically, similar to, but not identical with, his own rest state. And yet he was now awake and fully dressed. Surely that indicated —

And then the man turned, and the Nipe saw the weapon in the holster at his waist. There was a blinding instant of despair as he realized that his hopes had been shattered —

—and then he launched himself across the room.

Colonel Mannheim's hand darted toward the gun at his hip. It was purely reflex action. Even as he did it, he was aware that he would never get the weapon out in time to bring it to bear on the onrushing monster, and he was content that it should be so.

Twenty-five minutes later, the Nipe, after carefully licking off the fingers of his first pair of hands, went back into the hallway and headed down toward the sewers again.

The emotion he felt is inexpressible in human terms. Although he had not wished to kill the man, it cannot be said that the Nipe felt contrition. Although he had had no desire to harm the family, if any, of the late Colonel Mannheim, it cannot be said that the Nipe felt sadness or compassion.

Nor, again, although his stomachs churned and his body felt sluggish and heavy, can it be said that he felt any regret for what he had done.

That is not to say that he felt *no* emotion. He did. His emotions were as strong and as deep as those of a very sensitive human being. His emotions could bring him pain and they could bring him pleasure. They could crush him or exalt him. His emotions were just as real and as effective as any human emotions.

But they were *not* human emotions.

They were emotions, but not *human* emotions.

It is impossible to render into any human terms the simple statement: "The Nipe felt that he had properly rendered homage to a validly slain foe."

That cannot even begin to indicate the emotion the Nipe felt as he moved down toward the sewer and escape.

Captain Davidson Greer, his eyes staring with glassy hatred through the infra-red gunsight, was registering a very human emotion. His trigger fingers were twitching spasmodically-squeezing, squeezing, squeezing.

But his fingers were not on the triggers.

17

"It is not your fault, Bart," said George Yoritomo softly. "You had a perfect right to go."

Bart Stanton clenched his fists and turned suddenly to face the Japanese psychologist. "Sure! Hell, yes! We're not discussing my *rights*, George! We're discussing my criminal stupidity! I had the right to leave here any time I wanted to, sure. But I didn't have the right to exercise that right-if that makes any sense to you."

"It makes sense," Yoritomo agreed, "but it is not the way to look at it. You could not have been with the colonel every minute of every day. There was no way of knowing —"

"Of course not!" Stanton cut in angrily. "But I should have been there *this* time. He wanted me there, and I was gone. If I'd been there, he'd be alive at this moment."

"Possibly," Yoritomo said, "and then again, possibly not. Sit down over there on your bed, my young friend, and listen to me. Sit! That's it. Take a deep breath, hold it, and relax. I want your ears functioning when I talk to you. That's better.

"Now. I do not know where you went. That is your business. All you —"

"I went to Denver," Stanton said.

"And you found?"

"Nothing," Stanton said. "Absolutely nothing."

"What were you looking for?"

"I don't know. Something about my past. Something about myself. I don't know."

"Ah. You went to look up your family. You were trying to fill the holes in your memory. Eh?"

"Yes."

"And you did not succeed."

"No. No. There wasn't anything there that I didn't remember. In general, I mean. I found the files in the Bureau of Statistics. I know how my father died now, and how my mother died. And what happened to my brother. But all that didn't tell me anything. I'm still looking for something, and I don't know what it is. I was stupid to have gone. I suppose I should have asked you or Dr. Farnsworth or the colonel."

"But you thought we wouldn't answer," Yoritomo said.

"I guess that's about it. I should have asked you."

Yoritomo shook his head. "Not necessarily. It was actually better that you looked for yourself. Besides, we could not have given you any answer if you yourself do not know the question. We still can't."

"I have a feeling," Stanton said, "that you know the question as well as the answer."

"Perhaps. Perhaps not. But there are some things that every man must find out for himself. You were right to do as you did. If you had asked Colonel Mannheim for permission, he would have let you go. He would not have asked you to go to Government City with him. We —"

"That's the whole damned trouble!" Stanton snapped. "I'm the star boarder around here, the indispensable man. So I'm babied and I'm coddled, and when I goof off I'm patted on the back."

"And just how did you goof off?" Yoritomo asked.

"I should have been here, ready to go with the colonel."

"Very well. Suppose you had gone. Do you think you could have saved his life? He could have saved his own life if he'd wanted to. Instead, he specifically ordered the guard not to shoot under any circumstances. If you had been there, the results would have been the same. He would have forbidden you to do anything at all. The time is not yet ripe for you to face the Nipe. You would not have been able to protect him without disobeying his orders."

"I might have done just that," said Stanton.

Yoritomo was suddenly angry. "Then it is better that you were in Denver, young fool! Colonel Walther Mannheim believed that no single human life is worth the loss of the knowledge in that alien's mind! He proved that by sacrificing his own life when that became necessary. I like to think that I would have done the same thing myself. I am certain Dr.

Farnsworth would. We would rather *all* be dead than allow that fund of data to be lost to the rest of humanity!"

"But-but who will carry on, with him dead?" Stanton asked. "He was the one who co-ordinated everything. You and Farnsworth aren't cut out for that sort of thing. Nor am I."

"No," Yoritomo said. "But that has already been taken care of. Mannheim had a replacement ready. A message is being sent out in Mannheim's name, since we are keeping the colonel's death secret for the time being. *You* are the only indispensable man, Stanton. The rest of us can easily be replaced. The lives of dozens of human beings have been sacrificed-five years of your own life have been sacrificed-to put you in the right place at the right time. And the job you are to do does not and never has included acting as bodyguard for Colonel Mannheim or anyone else. Understand?"

Stanton nodded slowly. "I understand, George. I understand."

18

The detective pushed his way out of the crowded courtroom before the rest of the crowd started to move. The members of the jury were still filing in, and he knew that no one else would leave the room until the verdict was in.

He didn't care. He knew what the verdict ought to be. He knew also that juries had occasionally been swayed by histrionics on the part of the defense counsel, and had been persuaded to free guilty men. He knew, too, that prosecutors had railroaded innocent men. But such things as that didn't happen often in the Belt. A man doesn't live too long in the Belt unless he's capable of recognizing Truth when he sees it.

But even if the wrong verdict had been brought in, there would have been nothing he could do about it now. He had done his part. He had done everything he could. He had brought them in. He had testified. All the rest of it was up to the Jury and the Court-those two enigmatic halves of Justice and Judgment.

The point was that this was the perfect time to leave the courtroom. When he reached his office, he could, if he wanted-and, he thought ruefully, he probably *would* want to, in spite of his pretended indifference-call up to find out what the verdict had been. But, during these few moments, all eyes were on the jury box. No one was watching who left quietly by the side door of the big courtroom.

He moved silently and with assurance in the fractional-gee field of the planetoid. One of the uniformed guards looked at him and smiled, throwing him an informal salute.

The detective returned both. "If any of those news reporters ask which way I went," he said amiably, "tell 'em I went thataway." He gestured over his shoulder with a thumb.

"I ain't even seen you, Mr. Martin," said the guard.

The detective waved his thanks and kept going. It wasn't that he disliked newsmen. Most of them were fairly intelligent, pleasant people. But he didn't want to be asked any questions right now. He had given them interviews aplenty during the trial, and they could use those, now that the end of the trial had lifted the news ban. They had plenty of quotations from Stan Martin without asking him what he thought of the verdict itself.

Ten minutes later, he was in his own office in the Lloyd's Area. Helen, his secretary, was just cutting off the phone as he walked into the outer office. She flashed him a big smile.

"They just gave the verdict, Mr. Martin! Guilty all the way down the line-conspiracy, extortion, kidnapping, and all the others. The only 'not guilty' verdict was a minor one. They decided that Hedgepeth wasn't involved in the actual kidnapping itself, and therefore wasn't guilty of the physical assault of the guard."

"They're probably right," the detective said, "but, as you said, it's a minor point. It doesn't much matter whether he was physically present at the time the boy was taken or not; he was certainly in on the plot." He paused, frowning. "That's over and done with, except for a possible appeal. And it's unlikely that that would involve us, anyway. Get Mr. Pelham on the phone, will you? I'll take it in my office."

"The *Morton* case?" she asked.

"Yeah. There's something fishy about the wreck of the spaceship *Morton*, and I want Pelham to let me work on it."

He went on into his office and had barely sat down when the phone hummed. "Yes?" he said, depressing the switch.

"Mr. BenChaim would like to speak to you, sir," Helen said formally.

"Oh?" In order to have gotten here so quickly, BenChaim, too, must have left before the verdict was delivered. He was hardly more than a minute behind the detective. And that was unusual in a man who was waiting at the trial of the kidnappers of his own son. Still, Moishe BenChaim was an unusual man.

"Tell him to come right on in," the detective said. "Oh, and Helen ... hold off on that Pelham call for a little while." He didn't want to be talking business while BenChaim was in the office.

"Yes, sir," she said.

A few seconds later, the door opened, and Moishe BenChaim came in. He was not a big man, but he was broad of shoulder and broad of girth, built like a wrestler. He had a heavy, graying beard, and wore it with a patriarchal air. He was breathing rather heavily as he came through the door, and he stopped suddenly to pull a handkerchief from his pocket. He began coughing-harsh, racking, painful coughs that shook his heavy frame.

"Sorry," he said after a moment. "Damn lungs. Shouldn't try to move so fast." He wiped his lips and put the handkerchief away.

The detective didn't say anything. He knew that Moishe BenChaim had injured his lungs eighteen years before. An accident in space had ruptured his spacesuit, and the explosive decompression that had resulted had almost killed him. He had saved his own life by holding the torn spot with one hand and turning up the air-tank valve full blast with the other. The rough patch job had held long enough for him to get back inside his ship, but his lungs had never been the same, and his eyes were eternally bloodshot from the ruptured and distended capillaries.

"I noticed you'd slipped out of the courtroom," he went on. "I hope you don't mind my following you."

"Of course not, Mr. BenChaim," the detective said. "Sit down."

BenChaim sat in the chair across the desk from the detective. "I didn't wait for the verdict," he said. "I knew the conviction was certain after you testified."

"Thanks. My secretary got the news just before you came in. Guilty straight across the board. But your son's testimony was a lot more telling than mine."

"Guilty," BenChaim repeated with satisfaction. "Naturally. What else? I admit my son's testimony was good," he continued; "Little Shmuela told his story like a little man up there in the witness-box. Never looked scared, never got mixed up. But Shmuela's testimony was your testimony too, Mr. Martin. If it hadn't been for you, he wouldn't be here to testify, for which I'm grateful to God." Then he leaned back and spread his hands apart in a gesture of dismissal.

"But that's all over and done with," he said. "I came about a different matter." Again he paused, as if picking his words carefully. "Do you know a man named Barnabas Nguma?"

"Nguma? Yes; I met him once. Why?"

"He was in the courtroom today. He came to see me just before court convened."

"Oh?" the detective said noncommittally.

"Yes. He claims to represent an organization on Earth which has been trying to hire you for a job there. Is that right?"

"That's right," the detective said warily. "What did he want with you?"

"Now, that's a funny thing," BenChaim said. "It seems that he's under the impression that you turned down his job to take on this kidnapping. Is that right?"

"Not exactly," the detective said tightly. "I was working on your son's case before he and a couple of other men came out here to talk to me. But they'd written to me long before that." He wondered what BenChaim was getting at. He didn't owe any explanations to the industrialist, but, on the other hand, he couldn't be impolite to him.

"I see," BenChaim said, nodding his head slowly. "Like most Earthies, Mr. Nguma is suffering under a misapprehension. He seems to think that I have some sort of hold over you, that I was the one who made you turn down his job, so that you'd take *my* case."

"Oh? Was he angry because you'd put your own selfish interests ahead of his unselfish ones?" the detective asked with a trace of hard sarcasm in his voice.

"Oh, no," said BenChaim. "Oh, no. Not at all. He said he understood perfectly. But he wondered if, now that my boy had been returned safely, I might not put a little pressure on you to get you to take his case."

"And what did you say?"

Moishe BenChaim scowled. "I told him exactly where he could head in. I told him that I had no power over you whatever, that I hadn't hired you at all, that I didn't even know that you were working on the case until after you rescued Shmuel. I told him that even if I held the power of life and death over you I would never lift so much as a finger against you. I told him that it was just the other way around, in fact. I told him that you have such a power over me because of what you did for Shmuel that it is *I* who will jump through *your* hoop if ordered, not the other way around. I was quite angry." BenChaim relaxed a little before going on. "Actually, I'm sorry I blew up. He's a well-meaning man, I think."

"No doubt," the detective said. "Did he tell you what the job was?"

"With most heart-rending particulars," said BenChaim. "I was told all about how this Nipe has been killing and eating people, as if I didn't know already. But it wasn't until I heard him talk that I realized how scared people are back there on Earth. You know, Martin, we're insulated out here. We don't feel that terror, even when we read about it or see the reports on the newscasts. If everybody on Earth is as scared as that Mr. Nguma is, it's a wonder they haven't all panicked and taken to running around in circles."

"As a matter of fact, Mr. BenChaim," the detective said levelly, "they have begun to do just that. Mr. Nguma and his friends have been after me for a long time to take their job. They have pulled every trick they can think of-including this last one with you-to get me to go back to Earth and find that monster. I have refused them so often and so firmly that they are convinced I'm afraid to tackle the Nipe. They are convinced that I know I'll fail. And yet they keep after me. If that isn't running around in circles, it'll do until a better example comes along."

"They're out of their minds," BenChaim said flatly. "Of *course* no man in his right mind would try to face down that thing! It would be as silly as trying to outrun a bullet or do arithmetic faster than a computer. That's common sense. That's showing a healthy respect for the Nipe-not fear. At least, not fear in the way that those men are afraid."

Suddenly the detective knew why the industrialist had come. He knew that Moishe Ben-Chaim wanted to reassure Stanley Martin, to tell him that he was doing the sensible thing in turning down so dangerous an assignment. He could almost have predicted word for word what BenChaim was going to say next.

"Nguma may be here at any minute," said the industrialist. "He told me that he was going to come as soon as the trial was over. What are you going to tell him this time? I know it's none of my business, but I'm asking, just the same."

"I'm going to tell him *no*," the detective said. "I will not return to Earth for any reason whatever."

"Good," said BenChaim. "Good. That's the smart thing to do. And don't let him buffalo you. We know you out here in the Belt, Martin. I've been out here for thirty years, and I know what kind of guts it takes to do the things you've done. Those men don't understand space. Nobody understands space until he's lived in it and worked in it, and had cold death only a fraction of an inch away from his skin for hours and days at a time. No matter what those Earthies say, we know you've got more guts than anybody else in the Belt-to say nothing of those stay-at-homes on Earth."

"Thank you. I appreciate that," the detective said. But they were only words. He knew that BenChaim meant exactly what he said-or thought he meant it. But he also knew that BenChaim and others would always wonder why he had turned the job down.

God! he thought, *I wish I knew!* The thought was only momentary. Then, as it had done so many times before, his mind veered away from the dangerous subject.

Moishe BenChaim stood up. "Well, that's all I had to say, Mr. Martin. I just wanted to warn you that that man might be coming around and to tell you how I felt. Remember what I said about jumping through a hoop. Any time you need me, for anything at all, you just say so. Understand?"

"I understand," the detective said, forcing a smile. He rose and shook the industrialist's outstretched hand. "And thanks again," he added.

After BenChaim had gone, the detective sat thinking, toying with a pencil on his desk. Moishe BenChaim, like so many others in the Belt, had come out with nothing but his brain and his two hands and the equipment necessary to keep him alive. In thirty years, he had parlayed that into one of the biggest fortunes in the Solar System. It was men like that whose respect he valued, and, on the surface, he apparently had that respect. But refusing the Nipe job would dull the bright sheen of that respect, and he knew it. BenChaim had talked about how foolish it would be to try to beat the Nipe in a face-to-face encounter, but he hadn't meant it. He knew perfectly well that all Stanley Martin would be expected to do would be to find out where the Nipe's hideout was. Once that had been accomplished, men and machines-most especially machines-could wipe the monster from the face of the Earth. One well-placed bomb would do it, if the authorities only knew where to place that bomb. If only —

THE OPERATION IS ABOUT TO BEGIN. I NEED THE OTHER HALF OF MY FORCEPS. COME HOME AND JOIN THE BIG PARADE.

MANNHEIM

It took a second for the words to really impress themselves on his mind. He read them over again.

And the veil began to drop from the closed-off part of his mind.

Memories began to swarm back into his mind-memories that had been walled off and kept away from his conscious mind by the hypnotic suggestion implanted so long ago.

Oddly, it did not surprise or shock him. He was an expert at hypnosis, especially self-hypnosis. He recognized the message for exactly what it was: a series of code phrases designed to break the blockage that had been placed in his mind.

His only reaction was to laugh aloud. "By God!" he said. "It worked! It actually worked! Nearly six years, and I never suspected once!"

The phone hummed. He switched it on. "Mr. Pelham is on the phone, Mr. Martin," Helen said.

He watched as the florid, smiling face of Pelham, his superior, appeared on the screen. "What can I do for you, Martin?" he asked.

"I have a favor to ask, Mr. Pelham."

"Anything within reason," Pelham said. "After this BenChaim affair, you're in good standing around here." He chuckled.

"I want a leave of absence," the detective said.

Pelham looked a little surprised. "Well, I guess you deserve it. You need a rest, I imagine."

"No," the detective said. "No, it isn't that. I'm going after bigger game, is all."

"What's that?"

"I'm going to Earth to find the Nipe."

Again his mind veered away, refusing to consider the Nipe too carefully or too closely.

The intercom on his desk hummed, and he pressed the switch.

"Yes, Helen?"

"That Mr. Nguma was here while Mr. BenChaim was with you, Mr. Martin. I followed your instructions and told him that you would not see him."

"Fine. Thanks, Helen."

"Also, there's a radiogram for you from Earth."

"If it's from one of Nguma's colleagues," the detective said, "I don't want to see it. File it in the cylindrical file-under W."

"I don't think it is," the secretary said doubtfully. "I can't make any sense out of it. I'd better bring it in."

"Okay. And then put that call through to Pelham. I want to get going on that *Morton* spaceship wrecking. I'm getting itchy for action."

She brought in the radiogram and put it on his desk before calling Pelham. She had already read it, of course. It was her job to read such things.

The detective picked up the sheet of paper and read it.

19

From the very moment he had heard that "Stanley Martin" had arrived to take charge of the project, Bart Stanton pushed all thoughts of his brother out of his mind. He had fouled up once by thinking of himself rather than thinking of what had to be done; he would not make that mistake again.

Nor, apparently, did Martin have any desire to meet Bart Stanton. He took control of the project smoothly. Apparently Mannheim had taken into account the possibility of his own death and had arranged things accordingly. Although Martin was not a member of the World Police, his own record showed that he had the ability to handle the job, and an Executive Session had unanimously accepted Colonel Mannheim's wishes in the matter. There was little else they could do; the very fact that Mannheim had died in the way he had, ordering the guard to hold his fire, had stilled those voices on the Executive Council who had been wavering before.

Martin had come in to Earth almost secretly, without fanfare, and the general public was totally unaware that anything at all had happened.

Special messages, going through the channels known to be tapped by the Nipe, said that it would not be in the public interest to admit that the Nipe could actually penetrate the defenses of World Police Headquarters, so the Nipe was not surprised when the public news channels announced quietly that Colonel Walther Mannheim, the man who had been decorated twelve years before for the quelling of the Central Brazilian Insurrection, had died peacefully in his sleep. The funeral was quiet, but with full honors.

Stanton stopped worrying about such things. Until he had done the job that he had been rebuilt for, he was determined to make that goal his sole purpose. As the weeks sped by, he kept determinedly to his regime, exercising regularly to keep himself in top physical condition, and studying the three-dimensional motion studies of the Nipe in action.

Only one of these made him ill the first time he watched it, but it was the only recording of the Nipe actually in the process of killing a man, so he watched, over and over again, the shots taken from the gun tower when the Nipe attacked Colonel Mannheim.

A full-sized mockup of the Nipe's body had been built, with the best approximation possible of the Nipe's bone structure and musculature, and Stanton worked with it to determine what, if any, were the Nipe's physical limitations.

His only periods of relative relaxation occurred when he discussed the psychological peculiarities of the Nipe mind with George Yoritomo.

One afternoon, after a particularly strenuous boxing session, he walked into Yoritomo's office with a grin on his face. "I've been considering the problem of the apparent paradox of a high technology in a ritual-taboo system."

Yoritomo grinned back delightedly and waved Stanton to a chair. "Excellent! It is always much better if the student thinks these things out for himself. Now, while I fill this hand-furnace with tobacco and fire up, you will please explain to me all about it."

Stanton sat down and settled himself comfortably. "All right. In the first place, there's the notion of religion. In tribal cultures, the religion is usually-uh-animistic, I think the word is."

Yoritomo nodded silently.

"They believe there are spirits everywhere," Stanton said. "That sort of belief, it seems to me, would grow up in any race that had imagination, and the Nipes must have had plenty of that, or they wouldn't have the technology that we know they do have. Am I on the right track?"

"Very good. *Very* good," Yoritomo said in approval. "But what evidence have you that this technology was not given to them by some other, more advanced race?"

"I hadn't thought of that." Stanton stared into space for a moment, then nodded his head. "Of course. It would take too long to teach them. It wouldn't be worth all the trouble it would take to make them unlearn their fallacies and learn the new facts. It would take generations to do it unless this hypothetical other race killed off all the adult Nipes and started the little ones off fresh. And that didn't happen, because if it had, the ritual-taboo system would have died out, too. So that other-race theory is out."

"The argument is imperfect," Yoritomo said, "but it will suffice for the moment. Go on about the religion."

"Okay. Religious beliefs are not subject to pragmatic tests. That is, the spiritual beliefs aren't. Any belief that *could* be disproven by such a test would eventually die out. But beliefs in ghosts or demons or angels or life after death aren't disprovable by material tests, any more than they are provable. So, as a race increases its knowledge of the physical world, its religion would tend to become more and more spiritual."

"Agreed. Yes. It happened so among human beings," said Yoritomo. "But how do you link this fact with ritual-taboo?"

"Well, once a belief gains a foothold," Stanton said, "it is very difficult to wipe it out, even among human beings. Among Nipes, it would be well-nigh impossible. Once a code of ritual and of social behavior had been set up, it became permanent."

"For example?" Yoritomo urged.

"Well, shaking hands, for example," Stanton said after a pause. "We still do that, even if we don't have it fixed solidly in our heads that we *must* do it. I suppose it would never occur to a Nipe not to perform such a ritual."

"Just so," Yoritomo agreed vigorously. "Such things, once established in the minds of the race, would tend to remain. But it is a characteristic of a ritual-taboo system that it resists change. Change is evil. Change is wrong. We must use what we know to be true, not try something that has never been tried before. In a ritual-taboo system, a thing which is not ritual is, *ipso facto*, taboo. How, then, can we account for their high technological achievements?"

"The pragmatic engineering approach, I imagine," Stanton said. "If a thing works, then go ahead and use it. It is usable. If not, it isn't."

"Approximately," said Yoritomo. "But only approximately. Now it is my turn to lecture." He put his pipe in an ashtray and held up a long, bony finger. "Firstly, we must remember that the Nipe is equipped with a functioning imagination. Secondly, he has in his memory a tremendous amount of data, all ready at hand. He is capable of working out theories in his head, you see. Like the ancient Greeks, he finds no need to test such theories —*unless* his thinking indicates that such an experiment would yield something useful. Unlike the Greeks, he has no aversion to experiment. But he sees no need for useless experiment, either.

"Oh, he would learn, yes. But once a given theory proved workable, how resistant he would be to a new theory. Innovators, even in our own culture, have a very hard time working against the great inertia of a recognized theory. How much harder it would be in a ritual-taboo society with a perfect memory! How long-how *incredibly* long-it would take such a race to achieve the technology the Nipe now has!"

"Hundreds of thousands of years," said Stanton.

Yoritomo shook his head briskly. "Puh! Longer! Much longer!" He smiled with satisfaction. "I estimate that the Nipe race first invented the steam engine not less than ten million years ago!"

He kept smiling into the dead silence that followed.

After a long minute, Stanton said: "What about atomic energy?"

"At least two million years ago," Yoritomo said. "I do not think they have had the interstellar drive more than some fifty thousand years."

"No wonder our pet Nipe is so patient," Stanton said with a touch of awe in his voice. "How long do you suppose their individual life-span is?"

"Not so long, in comparison," said Yoritomo. "Perhaps no longer than our own at the least, or perhaps as much as five hundred years. Considering the tremendous handicaps against them, they have done quite well, I think. Quite well, indeed, for a race of illiterate cannibals."

"How's that again?" Stanton realized that the scientist was quite serious.

"Hadn't it occurred to you, my friend, that they must be cannibals?" Yoritomo asked. "And that they must be very nearly illiterate?"

"No," Stanton admitted, "it hadn't."

"The Nipe, like man, is omnivorous," Yoritomo pointed out. "Specialization tends to lead any race up a blind alley, and dietary restrictions are a particularly pernicious form of specialization. A lion would starve to death in a wheat field. A horse would perish in a butcher shop full of steaks. A man will survive as long as there is something around to eat-even if it's another man."

Yoritomo picked up his pipe and began tapping the ashes out of it. "Also," he went on, "we must remember that Man, early in his career of becoming top dog on Earth, began using a method of removing the unfit. Ritual traces of it remain today in some societies-the Jewish Bar Mitzvah, for instance, or the Christian Confirmation. Before and immediately after the Holocaust, there were still primitive societies on Earth-in New Guinea, for instance-which still made a rather hard ordeal out of the Rite of Passage, the ceremony whereby a boy becomes a man-if he passes the tests."

Yoritomo was filling his pipe, a look of somber satisfaction on his lean face. "A few millennia ago, a boy who underwent those tests was killed outright if he failed. And was eaten. He had not shown the ability to overrule with reason his animal instincts. Therefore, he was not a human being, but an animal. What better use for a young and succulent animal than to provide meat for the common larder?"

"And you think the same process must have been used by the Nipes?" Stanton asked.

Yoritomo nodded vigorously as he applied a match flame to the tobacco in his pipe. "The Nipe race must, of necessity, have had some similar ritualistic tests or they would not have become what they are," he said when he had puffed the pipe alight. "And we have already agreed that once the Nipes adopted something of that kind, it remained with them. Not so? Yes.

"Also, it can be considered extremely unlikely that the Nipe civilization-if such it can be called-has any geriatric problem. No, indeed. No old-age pensions, no old folks' homes, no senility. No, nor any specialists in geriatrics, either. When a Nipe becomes a burden because of age, he is ritually murdered and eaten with all due solemnity."

Yoritomo pointed his pipestem at Stanton. "Ah. You frown, my friend. Have I made them sound heartless, without the finer feelings of which we humans are so proud? Not so. When Junior Nipe fails his puberty tests, when Mama and Papa Nipe are sent to their final reward, I have no doubt that there is sadness in the hearts of their loved ones as the honored T-bones are passed around the table."

He put the pipe back in his mouth and spoke around it. "My own ancestors, not too far back, performed a ritual suicide by disemboweling themselves with a long, sharp knife. Across the abdomen —so! —and up into the heart —so! It was considered very bad form to faint or die before the job was done. Nearby, a relative or a close friend stood with a sharp sword, to administer the *coup de grace* by decapitation. It was all very sad and very honorable. Their loved ones bore the sorrow with great pride."

His voice, which had been low and tender, suddenly became very brisk. "Thank goodness it has gone out of fashion!"

"But how can you be *sure* they're cannibals?" Stanton asked. "Your argument sounds logical enough, but you can't be basing your theory on that alone."

"True! True!" Yoritomo jabbed the air twice with a rapid forefinger. "Evidence for such a theory would be most welcome, would it not? Very well, I give you the evidence. He eats human beings, our Nipe."

"That doesn't make him a cannibal," Stanton objected.

"Not *strictly*, perhaps. But consider. The Nipe is not a monster. He is not a criminal. No. He is a gentleman. He always behaves as a gentleman. He is shipwrecked on an alien planet. Around him, he sees evidence in profusion that ours is a technological society. But that is a contradiction! A paradox!

"For *we* are not civilized! No! We are not rational! We are not sane! We do not obey the Laws; we do not perform the Rituals. We are animals. Apparently intelligent animals, but animals nevertheless. How can this be?

"*Ha!* says the Nipe to himself. These animals must be ruled over by Real People. It is the only explanation. Not so?"

"Colonel Mannheim mentioned that," Stanton said. "Are you implying that the Nipe thinks there are other Nipes around, running the world from secret hideouts, like the villains in a Fu Manchu novel?"

"Not quite," said Yoritomo, laughing. "The Nipe is not at all incapable of learning something new. In point of fact, he is quite good at it, as witness the fact that he has learned many Earth languages. He picked up Russian in less than eight months simply by listening and observing. Like our own race, his undoubtedly evolved a great many languages during the beginnings of its progress-when there were many tribes, separated and out of communication with each other. It would not surprise me to find that most of these languages have survived and that our distressed astronaut knows them all. A new language would not bother him in the least.

"Nor would strangely shaped intelligent beings make him unhappy. His race should be aware, by now, that such things must exist. But it is very likely that he equates *true* intelligence with technology, and I do not think it likely that he has ever met a race higher than the barbarian level before. Such races were not, of course, human-by his definition. They showed possibilities, perhaps, but they had not by any means evolved far enough. And, considering the time span involved in their own progress toward a technological civilization, it is not at all unlikely that the Nipe thinks of technology as something that evolves in a race in the same way that intelligence does-or the body itself.

"So it would not surprise him to find that the Real People of this system were humanoid in shape instead of-ah-Nipoid? A bad word, but it will do for the nonce. To find Real People of a different shape is something new, but he can absorb it because it does not contradict anything he *knows.*

"But —! Any truly intelligent being that did not obey the Law and follow the Ritual *would* be a contradiction in terms. For our Nipe has no notion of a Real Person without those charac-teristics. Without those characteristics, technology is, of course, utterly impossible. Since he sees technology all around him, it follows that there must be Real People around somewhere that have those characteristics. Anything else is unthinkable."

"It seems to me that you're building an awfully involved theory out of pretty flimsy stuff," Stanton said.

Yoritomo shook his head. "Not at all. Not at all. Every scrap and shred of evidence we have points toward it. Why, do you suppose, does the Nipe conscientiously devour his victims, often risking his own safety to do so? Why do you suppose he never uses any weapon but his own hands to kill with?"

Yoritomo leaned forward and speared out at Stanton with a long, bony forefinger. "Why? To tell the Real People that he is a gentleman!"

He sat back with a satisfied smile and puffed complacently at his pipe, remaining silent while Bart Stanton considered his last remark.

"Just one thing," Stanton said after a minute. "It seems to me that he would be able to judge that some races have different Laws and Rituals than he does. Wouldn't they have a science comparable to our anthropology?"

Yoritomo grinned. "Nipology, shall we say? Well, he might, but it would not tell him what our anthropology tells us.

"Consider. How have we learned much of our knowledge of the early history of Man? By the study of ritual-taboo cultures. The so-called 'primitive' cultures. It is from these tribes that we have learned the multifarious ways in which a group of human beings can evolve a culture and a society. But does the Nipe have any such other tribes to study?"

"Why wouldn't he?" Stanton asked.

"Because there are none," Yoritomo said. "How could there be? Consider again. Once a race has evolved a fairly high technological level, it is capable of wiping out races which have not achieved that level. If the technologically advanced tribe is still at the ritual-taboo level, it will consider that all tribes which do not use the same Laws and Rituals as it does must be animals-dangerous animals that must be wiped out. Take a look at the history of our own race. In a few short centuries, we find that the technologically advanced civilization and culture of Renaissance Europe has spread over the whole globe. By military, economic, and religious conquest, it has, in effect, westernized the majority of Mankind.

"The same process would take place on the Nipe's world, only more thoroughly. The weaker tribes would vanish, the stronger would amalgamate."

"That process would take a lot of time," Stanton said.

"Indeed! Oh, yes, indeed," Yoritomo agreed. "But they have had the time, have they not? Eh? What Western European Man has partially achieved in less than a thousand years, surely the Nipe equivalent could have achieved in ten thousand thousand. Eh?"

"But I'd think that the Nipe would have realized, after ten years, that there is no such race of Real People," Stanton said. "He's had access to our records and books and such things. Or does he reject them all as lies?"

"Possibly he would, if he could read them," Yoritomo said. "Did I not say he was illiterate?"

"You mean he's learned to speak our languages, but not to read them?"

The psychologist smiled broadly. "Your statement is accurate, my friend, but incomplete. It is my opinion that the Nipe is incapable of reading any written language whatever. The concept does not exist in his mind, except vaguely."

Stanton closed one eye and gave Yoritomo the glance askance. "Aw, come *awwn*, George! A technological race without a written language? That's impossible!"

"Ah, no. No, it isn't. Ask yourself: What need has a race with a perfect memory for written records? At least, in the sense that we think of them. Certainly not to remember things. What would a Nipe need with a memorandum book or a diary? All of their history and all of their technology exists in the collective mind of the race.

"Think, for a moment, of their history. If it is somewhat analogous to human history-and, as we have seen, there is reason to believe that this is so-then we can, in a way, trace the development of writing. We —"

"Wait a minute!" Stanton held up his hand. "I think I see what you're driving at."

"Ah. So?" Yoritomo nodded. "Very well. Then *you* expound."

"I can give it to you in two sentences," Stanton said. "One: Their first writing was probably pictographic and was learned only by a select priestly class. Two: It still is."

"Ahhhh!" Yoritomo's eyes lit up. "Admirable! Most admirable! And succinctly put, too. And, to top it off, almost precisely correct. That is what happened here on Earth; are we wrong in assuming that such may have happened elsewhere in the Universe? (Remembering always, my dear Bart, that we must not make the mistake of thinking like our friend, the Nipe, and assuming that everybody else in the Universe has to be like us in all things.)

"You are correct. That is why I hedged when I said he was *almost* illiterate. There is a possibility that a written symbology does exist for Nipes. But it is used almost entirely for ritualistic purposes, it is pictographical in form, and is known only to a very few. For others to learn it would be taboo.

"Remember, I said that there is only one society, one culture remaining on the Nipe planet. And remember that history is a very late development in our own culture, just as written language is. One important event in every ten centuries of Nipe history would still give a Nipe historian ten thousand events to remember just since the invention of the steam engine. What, then, does Nipe history become? A series of folk chants, of *chansons de geste*."

"Why?" Stanton asked. "If they have perfect memories, why would histories be distorted?"

"Time, my dear boy. Time." Yoritomo spread his hands in a gesture of futility. "When one has a few million years of history to learn, it *must* become distorted, even in a race with a perfect memory. Otherwise, no individual would have a chance to learn it all in a single lifetime, even a lifetime of five hundred years, much less to pass that knowledge on to another. So only the most important events are reported. And that means that each historian must also be an editor. He must excise those portions which he considers unimportant."

"But wouldn't that very limitation induce them to record history?" Stanton asked. "Right there is your inducement to use a written language."

Yoritomo looked at him with wide-eyed innocence. "Why? *What good is history?*"

"Ohhh," said Stanton. "I see."

"Certainly you do," Yoritomo said firmly. "Of what use is history to the ritual-taboo culture? Only to record what is to be done. And, with a memory that can *know* what is to be done, of what use is a historian, except to remember the *important* things. No ritual-taboo culture looks upon history as we do. Only the doings of the great are recorded. All else must be edited out. Thus, while the memory of the individual may be, and *is*, perfect, the memory of the race is not. *But they don't know that!*"

"What about communications, then?" Stanton asked. "What did they use before they invented radio?"

"Couriers," Yoritomo said. "And, possibly, written messages from one priestly scribe to another. That last, by the way, has probably survived in a ritualistic form. When an officer is appointed to a post, let's say, he may get a formal paper that says so. The Nipes may use symbols to signify rank and so on. They must have a symbology for the calibration of scientific instruments.

"But none of these requires the complexity of a written language. I dare say our use of it is quite baffling to him.

"For teaching purposes, it is quite unnecessary. Look at what television and such have done in our own civilization. With such tools as that at hand-recordings and pictures-it is possible to teach a person a great many things without ever teaching him to read. A Nipe certainly wouldn't need any aid for calculation, would he? We humans must use a piece of paper to multiply two ten-digit numbers together, but that's because our memories are faulty. A Nipe has no need for such aids."

"Are you really positive of all this, George?" Stanton asked.

Yoritomo shrugged. "How can we be absolutely positive at this stage of the game? Eh? Our evidence is sketchy, I admit. It is not as solidly based as our other reconstructions of his background, but it appears that he thinks of symbols as being unable to convey much information. The pattern for his raids, for instance, indicates that his knowledge of the materials he wants and their locations comes from vocal sources-television advertising, eavesdropping on shipping orders, and so on. In other words, he cases the joint by ear. If he could understand written information, his job would be much easier. He could find his materials much more quickly and easily. And, too, we have never seen him either read a word or write one. From this evidence, we are fairly certain that he can neither read nor write any terrestrial language-or even his own." He spread his hands again. "As I said, it is not proof."

"No," Stanton agreed, "but I must admit that the whole thing makes for some very interesting speculation, doesn't it?"

"Very interesting, indeed." Yoritomo folded his hands in his lap, smiled seraphically, and looked at the ceiling. "In fact, my friend, we are now so positive of our knowledge of the Nipe's mind that we are prepared to enter into the next phase of our program."

"Oh?" Stanton distinctly felt the back of his neck prickle.

"Yes," said Yoritomo. "Mr. Martin feels that if we wait much longer, we may run into the danger of giving the Nipe enough time to complete his work on his communicator." He looked at Stanton and chuckled, but there was no humor in his short laugh. "We would not wish our friend, the Nipe, to bring his relatives into this little tussle, would we, Bart?"

"That's been our deadline all along," Bart said levelly. "The object all along has been to let the Nipe work without hindrance as long as he did not actually produce a communicator that would-as you put it-bring his relatives into the tussle. Have things changed?"

"They have," Yoritomo acknowledged. "Why wouldn't they? We have been working toward that as a *final* deadline. If it appeared that the Nipe were actually about to contact his confederates out there somewhere, we would be forced to act immediately, of course. Plan Beta would go into effect. But we don't want that, do we?"

"No," said Stanton. "No." He was well aware what a terrible loss it would be for humanity if Plan Beta went into effect. The Nipe would have to be literally blasted out of his cozy little nest.

"No, of course not." Yoritomo chuckled again, with as little mirth as he had before. "Within a very short while, if we are correct, we shall, with your help, arrest the most feared arch-criminal that Earth has ever known. I dare say that the public will be extremely happy to hear of his death, and I know that the rest of us will be happy to know that he will never kill again."

Stanton suddenly saw the fateful day for which he had been so carefully prepared and trained looming terrifyingly large in the immediate future.

"How soon?" he asked in an oddly choked voice.

"Within days." Yoritomo lowered his eyes from the ceiling and looked into Stanton's face with a mild, bland expression.

"Tomorrow," he said, "the propaganda phase begins. We will announce to the world that the great detective, Stanley Martin, has come to Earth to rid us of the Nipe."

20

The arrival of the great Stanley Martin was a three-day wonder in the public news channels. His previous exploits were recounted, with embellishments, several times during the next seventy-two hours. The "arrival" itself was very carefully staged. A special ship belonging to the World Police brought him in, and he was met by four Government officials in civilian clothes. The entire affair was covered live by news cameras. No one on Earth suspected that he had been on Earth for weeks before; a few *knew* it, but it never even occurred to the rest.

Later, a special interview was arranged. Philip Quinn, a news interviewer who was noted for his deferential attitude toward those whom he had the privilege of interviewing, was chosen for the job.

Stanley Martin's dynamic, forceful personality completely overshadowed Quinn.

But in spite of all the publicity, not one word, not one hint about the method by which Stanley Martin intended to bring the Nipe in was released. There were all kinds of speculations, ranging from the mystically sublime to the broadly comical. One self-styled archbishop of a California nut cult declared that Martin was a saint appointed by God to exorcise the Demon Nipe that had been plaguing Mankind and that the Millennium was therefore due at any moment. He was, he said, sending Stanley Martin a sealed letter which contained a special exorcism prayer that would do the job very nicely. Why hadn't he used it himself? Because if anyone other than a saint or an angel used it, it would backfire on the user and destroy him. Naturally the archbishop did not claim himself to be a saint, but he knew that Martin was because he had plainly seen the halo around the detective's head when he saw him on TV.

An inventor in Palermo, Sicily, solemnly declared that he had sent Stanley Martin the plans for a device that would render him invisible to the Nipe and therefore make the Nipe easy to conquer. No, there was no danger that the device might fall into the wrong hands and be used by human criminals, since it did not render a person invisible to human eyes, only to Nipe eyes.

The first item was played up big in the newscasts. The second was quashed-fast! —for the very simple reason that the Nipe just might have believed it.

One note throbbed in the background of every interview with responsible persons. It was the unobtrusive note of a soft clarinet played in a great symphony, all the more telling because it was never played loudly or insistently, but it was there all the same. Whenever the question of the Nipe's actual whereabouts came up, the note seemed to ring a trifle more clearly, but never more loudly. That single throbbing note was the impression given by everyone who was interviewed, or who expressed any views on the subject, that the Nipe was hiding somewhere in the Amazonian jungles of South America. It was the last place on Earth that had still not been thoroughly explored, and it seemed to be the only place that the Nipe could hide.

Only a small handful of the vast array of people who were dispensing this carefully tailored propaganda knew what was going on. More than ninety-nine percent of the newsmen involved in the affair thought they were honestly giving the news as they saw it, and none of them saw the invisible but very powerful hand of Stanley Martin shifting the news just enough to give it the bias he wanted.

The comedians on the entertainment programs let the whole story alone for the most part. There were no clever skits, no farcical takeoffs on the subject of Stanley Martin and the Nipe. One comedian, who was playing the part of a henpecked husband, did remark: "If my wife gets any meaner, I'm going to send Stan Martin after *her*!" But it didn't get much of a laugh. And the Government organization had nothing to do with that kind of censorship; it was self-imposed. Every one of the really great comics recognized, either consciously or subconsciously, that the Nipe was not a subject for humor. Such jokes would have made them about as popular as the Borscht Circuit comedian who told a funny story about Dachau in 1946.

Aside from the subtle coloring given it by the small, Mannheim-trained group of propaganda experts, the news went out straight.

The detective himself, after that one single interview, vanished from sight. No one knew where he was, though, again, there were all kinds of speculations, all of them erroneous. Actually, he was a carefully guarded and willing prisoner in a suite in one of the big hotels in Government City.

On the fourth day, the big operation began without fanfare. The actual maneuvering to capture the alien that had terrorized a planet began shortly after noon.

At a few minutes before three that afternoon, the man whom the world knew as Stanley Martin suddenly suffered a dizzy spell and nearly fainted.

Then, almost like a child, he began to weep.

FINAL INTERLUDE

Colonel Walther Mannheim said: "It will take five years, Stanton."

He was looking at the young man seated in one of the three chairs in the small, comfortable room. There was a clublike atmosphere about the room, but none of the three men were relaxed.

"Five years?" said the young man. He looked at the third man.

Dr. Farnsworth nodded. "More or less. More if it's a partial failure-less if it's a complete failure."

"Then there *is* a chance of failure?" the young man asked.

"There is always a chance of failure in any major surgical undertaking," Dr. Farnsworth said. "Even in the most routine cases, things can go wrong. We're only men, Mr. Stanton. We're neither magicians nor gods."

"I know that, Doctor," the young man said. "Nobody's perfect, and I don't expect perfection. Can you give me a —an estimate on the chances?"

"I can't even give you any kind of guess," said Farnsworth. He smiled rather grimly. "So far, we have had no failures. Our mortality rate is a flat zero. We have never lost a patient because we've never had one. As I told you, this will be the first time the operation has ever been performed on a human being. Or, rather," he corrected himself, "I should say series of operations. This is not one single-er-cut-and-suture job, like an appendectomy."

"All right, then, call it a series of operations," the young man said. "I assume each of them has been performed individually?"

"Not exactly. Some of them have never been performed on any human being simply because they require not only special conditions, but they require that the steps leading up to them have already been performed."

"You don't make things sound very rosy, Doctor."

"I'm not trying to. I'm trying to give you the facts. Personally, I think we have a better than ninety percent chance of success. I wouldn't try it if I thought otherwise. With modern mathematical methods of analyzing medical theory, we can predict success for such an intricate series of operations. We can predict what will happen when massive doses of hormones and enzymes and such are used. But medicine still remains largely an art in spite of all that.

"In parallel operations, performed on primates, our results were largely successful. But remember that not even every human being has the genetic structure necessary to undergo this particular treatment, and a monkey's gene structure is quite different from yours or mine."

"I'll just ask you one question," the young man said firmly. "If *you* were being asked to undergo this treatment, would you do it?"

Dr. Farnsworth didn't hesitate. "All things considered, yes, I would."

"What do you mean, 'All things considered'?"

"The very fact that the Nipe exists, and that this is the only method of dealing with him that is even remotely possible would certainly influence my opinion," Farnsworth said. "I might not be so quick to go through it, frankly, if it were not for the fact that the future of the entire human race would depend upon my decision." He paused, then added: "I would hesitate to go through with it if there were no Nipe threat, not because I would be afraid that the operations might fail, but because of what I would be afterward."

"Um. Yes." The young man caught his lower lip between his teeth and thought for a moment. "Yes, I see what you mean. Being a lone superman in a world of ordinary people mightn't be so pleasant."

Colonel Mannheim, who had been sitting silently during the discussion between the two men, said: "Look, Stanton, I know this is tough. Actually, it's a lot tougher on you than it is on your brother, because *you* have to make the decision. *He* can't. But I want you to keep it in mind that there's nothing compulsory in this. Nobody's trying to force you to do anything."

There was a touch of bitterness in the young man's smile as he looked at the colonel. "No. You merely remind me of the fact and leave the rest to my sense of duty."

Colonel Mannheim, recognizing the slightly altered quotation, returned his smile and gave him the next line. "'Your sense of duty!'"

The bitterness vanished, and the young man's smile became a grin. "'Don't put it on that footing!'" he quoted back in a melodramatic voice. "'As I was merciful to you just now, be merciful to me! I implore you not to insist on the letter of your bond just as the cup of happiness is at my lips!'"

"'We insist on nothing,'" returned the colonel; "'we content ourselves with pointing out *your duty.*'"

Dr. Farnsworth had no notion of what the two of them were talking about, but he kept silent as he noticed the tension fading.

"'Well, you have appealed to my sense of duty,'" the young man continued, "'and my duty is all too clear. I abhor your infamous calling; I shudder at the thought that I have ever been mixed up with it; but duty is before all-at any price I will do my duty.'"

"'Bravely spoken!'" said the colonel. "'Come, you are one of us once more.'"

"'Lead on. I follow.'"

And the two of them broke out in laughter while Farnsworth looked on in total incomprehension. His was not the kind of mind that could face a grim situation with a laugh.

Even after he quit laughing, the smile remained on the young man's face. "All right, Colonel, you win. We'll go through with it, Martin and I."

"Good!" Mannheim said warmly. "Do you have the papers, Dr. Farnsworth?"

"Right here," Farnsworth said, opening a briefcase that was lying on the table. He was glad to be back in the conversation again. He took out a thick sheaf of papers and spread them on the table. Then he handed the young man a pen. "You'll have to sign at the bottom of each sheet," he said.

The young man picked up the papers and read through them carefully. Then he looked up at Farnsworth. "They seem to be in order. Uh-about Martin. You know what's the matter with him —I mean, aside from the radiation. Do you think he'll be able to handle his part of the job after-after the operations?"

"I'm quite sure he will. The operations, plus the therapy we'll give him afterward should put him in fine shape."

"Well." He looked thoughtful. "Five more years. And then I'll have the twin brother that I never really had at all. Somehow that part of it just doesn't really register, I guess."

"Don't worry about it, Stanton," said Dr. Farnsworth. "We have a complex enough job ahead of us without your worrying in the bargain. We'll want your mind perfectly relaxed. You have your own ordeal to undergo."

"Thanks for reminding me," the young man said, but there was a smile on his face when he said it. He looked at the release forms again. "All nice and legal, huh? Well ..." He hesitated for a moment, then he took the pen and wrote *Bartholomew Stanton* in a firm, clear hand.

21

Captain Davidson Greer sat in a chair before an array of TV screens, his gray-green eyes watchful. In the center of one of the screens, the Nipe's image sat immobile, surrounded by the paraphernalia in his hidden nest. Other screens showed various sections of the long tunnel that led south from the opening in the northern end of the island. At the captain's fingertips was a bank of controls that would allow him to switch from one pickup to another if necessary, so that he could see anything anywhere in the tunnels. He hoped that wouldn't be necessary. He did not want any of the action to take place anywhere but in the places where it was expected-but he was prepared for alterations in the plan. In other rooms, nearly a hundred other men were linked into the special controls that allowed them to operate the little rat spies that scuttled through the underground darkness, and the captain's system would allow him to see through the eyes of any one of those rats at an instant's notice.

The screen which he was watching at the moment, however, was not connected with an underground pickup. It was linked with a pickup in the bottom of a basketball-sized sphere driven by a small inertial engine that held the sphere hovering in the air above the game sanctuary on the northern tip of Manhattan Island. In the screen, he had an aerial view of the grassy, rocky mounds where the earth hid the shattered and partially melted ruins of long-collapsed buildings. In the center of the screen was a bird's-eye view of a man holding a rifle. He was walking slowly, picking his way carefully along the bottom of the shallow gully that had once been upper Broadway.

"Barbell," the captain said. A throat microphone picked up the words and transmitted them to the ears of the man in the screen. "Barbell, this is Barhop. There are no wild animals within sight, but remember, we can't see everything from up here, so keep your eyes open."

"Right, Barhop," said a rather muffled voice in the captain's ear.

"Fine. And if you do meet up with anything, shoot to kill." There were plenty of wild animals in the game sanctuary-some of them dangerous. Not all of the inhabitants of the Bronx Zoological Gardens had been killed on that day when the sun bomb fell. Being farther north, they had had better protection, and some of them, later, had wandered southward to the island. Captain Greer knew perfectly well that Stanton, bare-handed, was more than a match for a leopard or a lion, but he didn't want Stanton to tire himself fighting with an animal. The rifle would most likely never be used; it was merely another precaution.

It would have been possible, and perhaps simpler, to have taken Stanton to the opening by flyer, but that would have created other complications. Traffic rules forbade flyers to go over the game sanctuary at any altitude less than one thousand feet. One flyer, going in low, would have attracted the attention of the traffic police, and Stanley Martin wanted no attention whatever drawn to this area. Even the procedure of instructing the traffic officers to ignore one flyer would have attracted more attention than he wanted. They would have remembered those instructions afterward.

Stanton walked.

Captain Greer's eye caught something at the edge of the screen. It moved toward the center as the floating eye moved with Stanton.

"Barbell," the captain said, "there's a deer ahead of you. Just keep moving."

Stanton rounded the corner of a pile of masonry. He could see the animal now himself. The deer stared at the intruder for a few seconds, then bounded away with long, graceful leaps.

"Magnificent animal." It was Stanton's voice, very low. The remark wasn't directed toward anyone in particular. Captain Greer didn't answer.

The captain lit a cigarette and leaned back in his chair, his eyes on the screens. The Nipe still sat, unmoving. He was apparently in one of his "sleep" states. The captain wasn't sure that that was the blessing that it might have seemed. He had no way of knowing how much external disturbance it would take to "wake" the Nipe, and as long as he was sitting quietly, the chances were greater that he would hear movement in the tunnel. If he were active, his senses might be more alert, but he would also be distracted by his own actions and the noises he made himself.

It didn't matter, the captain decided. One way was as good as another in this case. The point was to get Stanton into an advantageous position before the Nipe knew he was anywhere around.

He looked back at the image of Stanton, a black-clad figure in a flexible, tough, skin-tight suit. The Nipe would have a hard time biting through that artificial hide, but it gave Stanton as much freedom as if he'd been naked.

Stanton knew where he was going. He had studied maps of the area, and had been taken on a vicarious tour of the route by means of the very flying eye that was watching him now. But things look different from the ground than from the air, and no amount of map study will familiarize a person with terrain as completely as an actual personal survey.

Stanton paused, and Captain Greer heard his voice. "Barhop, this is Barbell. Those are the cliffs up ahead, aren't they?"

"That's right, Barbell. You go up that slope to your left. The opening is in that pile of rock at the base of the cliff."

"They're higher than I'd thought," Stanton commented. Then he started walking again.

The tunnel entrance he was heading for had once been a wide opening, drilled laterally into the side of the cliff, and big enough to allow easy access to the tunnels, so that the passengers of those old underground trains could get to the platforms where they stopped. But the sun bomb had changed all that. The concussion had shaken loose rock at the top of the cliff and a minor avalanche had obliterated all indications of the tunnel's existence, except for one small, narrow opening near the top of what had once been a wide hole in the face of the cliff.

Stanton walked slowly toward the spot until he was finally at the base of the slope of rock created by that long-ago avalanche. "Up there?" he asked.

"That's right," said Captain Greer.

"I think I'll leave the rifle here, Barhop," Stanton said. "No point in carrying it up the slope."

"Right. Put it in those bushes to your left. They'll conceal it, won't they?"

"I think so. Yeah." Stanton hid the rifle and then began making his way up the talus slope.

Captain Greer flipped a switch. "Team One! He's coming in. Are those alarms deactivated?"

"All okay, Barhop," said a voice. "This is Leader One. I'll meet him at the hole."

"Right." Captain Greer reversed the switch again. "Are you ready, Barbell?"

Stanton looked into the dark hole. It was hardly big enough to crawl through, and ended in a seeming infinity of blackness. He took the special goggles from the case at his belt and put them on. Inside the hole, he saw a single rat, staring at him with beady eyes.

"I'm ready to go in, Barhop," Stanton said.

He got down on his hands and knees and began to crawl through the narrow tunnel. Ahead of him, the rat turned and began to lead the way.

22

The big tunnel inside the cliff was long and black, and the air was stale and thick with the stench of rodents. Stanton stood still for a minute, stretching his muscles. Crawling through that cramped little opening had not been easy. He looked around him, trying to probe the luminescent gloom that the goggles he wore brought to his eyes.

The tunnel stretched out before him-on and on. Around him was the smell of viciousness and death. Ahead...

It goes on to infinity, Stanton thought, *ending at last at zero.*

The rat paused and looked back, waiting for him to follow.

"Okay," Stanton muttered. "Let's go."

The rat led him down the long tunnel, deep into the cliffside, until at last they came to a stairway that led downward into the long tunnels where the trains had once run. They came to the platform where passengers had once waited for those trains. Four feet below the edge of the platform were the rusted tracks that had once borne those trains.

He lowered himself over the edge to stand on the rail.

"Barbell," said a voice in his ear, "Barhop here. Do you read?"

It was the barest whisper, picked up by the antennas in his shoes from the steel rail that ran along the floor of the dark tunnel.

"Read you, Barhop."

"Move out, then. You've got a long stroll to go."

Stanton started walking, keeping his feet near the rail, in case Greer wanted to call again. As he walked, he could feel the slight motion of the skin-tight woven suit that he wore rubbing gently against his skin.

And he could hear the scratching patter of the rats.

Mostly they stayed away from him, avoiding the strange being that had invaded their underground realm, but he could see them hiding in corners and scurrying along the sides of the tunnels, going about their unfathomable rodent business.

Around him, six rat-like remote-control robots moved with him, shifting their pattern constantly as they patrolled his moving figure.

Far ahead, he knew, other rat robots were stationed, watching and waiting, ready to deactivate the Nipe's detection devices at just the right moment. Behind him, another horde moved forward to turn the devices on again.

It had, he knew, taken the technicians a long time to learn how to shut off those detectors without giving the alarm to the Nipe's instruments.

There were nearly a hundred men in on the operation, controlling the robot rats or watching the hidden cameras that spied upon the Nipe. Nearly a hundred. And every single one of them was safe.

They were all outside the tunnel and far away. They were with Stanton only by proxy. They could not die here in this stinking hole, no matter what happened. But Stanton could.

There was no help for it, no other way it could be done. Stanton had to go in person. A full-sized robot proxy might be stronger, although not faster unless Stanton was at the controls, than the Nipe. But the Nipe would be able to tell that the thing was a robot, and he would simply destroy it with one of his weapons. A remote-control robot could never get close enough to the Nipe to do any good.

"We do not know positively," Dr. Yoritomo had said, "whether he would recognize it as a robot or not, but his instruments would show the metal easily enough, and his eyes would be able to tell him that the machine was not covered with human skin. The rats are small enough so that they can be made mostly of plastic, and they are covered with real rat hides. In addition, our friend, the Nipe, is used to seeing them around. But a human-sized robot? Ah, no. Never."

So Stanton had to go in person, walking southward along the tracks, through the miles of blackness that led to the nest of the Nipe.

Overhead was Government City.

He had looked out upon those streets only the night before, and he knew that only a short distance away there was an entirely different world.

Somewhere up there, his brother was waiting, after having run the gamut of publicity. He was a celebrity. "Stanley Martin, the greatest detective in the Solar System," they'd called him. Fine stuff, that. Stanton wondered what the asteroids were like. What would it be like to live out in space, where a man still had plenty of space to move around in and could fashion his life to suit himself? Maybe there would be a place in the asteroids for a hopped-up superman.

Or maybe there would only be a place here, beneath the streets of Government City, for a dead superman.

Not if I can help it, Stanton thought with a grim smile.

The walking seemed to take forever in one way, but, in another way, Stanton didn't mind it. He had a lot to think over. Seeing his brother's image on the TV had been unnerving yesterday, but today he felt as though everything had been all right all along.

His memory was still a long way from being complete, and it probably always would be, he thought. He could still scarcely recall any real memories of a boy named Martin Stanton, but-and he smiled a little at the thought-he knew more about him than his brother did, even so.

It made very little difference now. That Martin Stanton was gone. In effect, he had been demolished-what little there had been of him-and a new structure had been built on the old foundation.

And yet, it was highly probable that the new structure was very like that that would have developed naturally if the accident so early in Martin Stanton's life had never occurred.

Stanton kept walking. There was a timeless feeling about his march through the depths of the ground, as though every step through the blackness was exactly like every other step, and it was only the same step over and over again.

He skirted a pile of rubble on his right. There had been a station here, once; the street above had caved in and filled it with brick, concrete, cobblestones, and steel scrap, and then it had been sealed over when Government City was built.

A part of one wall was still unbroken, though. A sign built of tile said 125TH STREET, he knew, although it was hard to make it out in the dim glow. He kept on walking, ignoring the rats that scampered over the rubble.

A mile or so farther on, he whispered: "Barbell to Barhop. How's everything going?"

"Barhop to Barbell," came the answer. "No sign of any activity from Target. So far, none of the alarms have been triggered."

"What's he doing?" Stanton whispered. It seemed only right to keep his voice low, although he was fairly certain that his voice would not carry to the Nipe, even through these echoing tunnels. He was still miles away.

"He's still sitting motionless," said Captain Greer. "Thinking, I suppose. Or sleeping. It's hard to tell."

"All right. Let me know if he starts moving, will you?"

"Will do."

Poor unsuspecting beastie, Stanton thought. *Ten long years of hard work, of feeling secure in his little nest, and within a very short time he's going to get the shock of his life.*

Or maybe not. There was no way of knowing what kind of shocks the Nipe had taken in the course of his life, Stanton thought. There was no way of knowing whether the Nipe was even capable of feeling anything like shock, as a matter of fact.

It was odd, he thought, that he should feel a strong kinship toward both the Nipe and his brother in such similar ways. He had never met the Nipe, and his brother was only a dim picture in his old memories, but they were both very well known to him. Certainly they were better known to him than he was to them.

And yet, seeing his brother's face on the TV screen, hearing his voice, watching the way he moved about, watching the changing expressions on his face, had been a tremendously moving experience. Not until that moment, he thought, had he really known himself.

Meeting him face to face would be much easier now, but it would still be a scene highly charged with emotional tension.

His foot kicked something that rattled and rolled away from him. He stopped, freezing in his tracks, looking downward, trying to pierce the dully glowing gloom. The thing he had kicked was a human skull.

He relaxed and began walking again.

There were plenty of human bones down here. Mannheim had told him that the tunnels had been used as air-raid shelters when the sun bomb had hit the island during the Holocaust. Men, women, and children by the thousands had crowded underground after the warning had come-and they had died by the thousands when the bright, hot, deadly gases had roared down the ventilators and stairwells.

There were even caches of canned goods down here, some of them still perfectly sealed after all this time. The hordes of rats, wiser than they knew, had chewed at them, exposing the steel beneath the thin tin plate. And, after a while, oxidation would weaken the can to the point where some lucky rat could gnaw through the rusty spot and find himself a meal. Then he would move the empty can aside and begin gnawing at the next in line. He couldn't get through the steel, but he would scratch the tin off, and the cycle would begin again. Later, another rat would find that can weak enough to bite through. It kept the rats fed almost as well as an automatic machine might have.

The tunnel before him was an endless monochromatic world that was both artificial and natural. Here was a neatly squared-off mosaic of ceramic tile that was obviously man-made; over there, on a little hillock of earth, squatted a colony of fat mushrooms. In several places he had to skirt little pools of dark, stagnant water; twice he had to climb over long heaps of crumbling rust that had once been trains of subway cars.

He kept moving-one man, alone, walking through the dark toward a superhuman monster that had terrorized Earth for a decade.

A drug that would knock out the Nipe would have been very useful, but to synthesize such a drug would have required a greater knowledge of the biochemical processes of the Nipe than any human scientist had. The same applied to anesthetic gases, or electric shock, or supersonics. There was no way of determining how much would be required to knock him out or how much would be required to kill. There were no easy answers.

The only answer was a man called Stanton.

Boots! Boots! Boots! Boots! Marchin' up and down again!

And there's no discharge in the war!

Stanton hummed the song in his mind. It seemed that he had been walking forever through the Kingdom of Hades, while around him twittered the ghosts of the dead.

Poor shades, he thought, entertaining the fancy for a brief moment, *will I be one of you in a short while?*

There was no answer, though the squeaking continued. The sound of his feet and the snarling chirping of the rats were the only sounds in the world.

"Barhop to Barbell," said a voice suddenly, sounding very loud in his ear, "this is where you have to make your change to the other tunnel."

"Barbell to Barhop. I know. I've been watching the markers."

"Just precaution, Barbell," Captain Greer said. "How do you feel?"

"I'd like to rest for a few minutes, frankly," Stanton said.

"Feeling tired?" There was just the barest tinge of alarm in the captain's voice.

"No," Stanton said. "I just want to sit down and rest my feet for a few minutes."

There was a pause. Then the captain's voice came again. "Okay, go ahead and relax, Barbell. Take ten. But be ready to move fast if I yell. These alarm systems are tricky things to hold. And don't start moving again without letting me know."

"Right."

Stanton lifted himself out of the trench in which the tunnel ran and sat on the edge of the boarding platform. It wasn't far now. There was only one more of the old entranceways between himself and the Nipe. This particular one was a transfer point, where two different parts of the tunnel network met and it was possible to transfer from one to another. It required going up a couple of flights of stairs to the next higher level, and changing to another tunnel going southward.

There were other ways. This tunnel, the one he had been following for so long, branched a little farther south. If he took one branch, he would end up to the east of the Nipe; the other would bring him to a point on the west. From either, he would have to travel laterally through another set of tunnels, but neither route offered anything that this one didn't have, and the most direct route would be best.

"Barbell to Barhop," he whispered, "I'm ready to go."

"It's only been five minutes."

"I know. But I rest pretty fast, too. Let's move out."

There were a few seconds of silence, then Captain Greer said: "All set, Barbell. Move out."

Stanton got to his feet and walked toward the stairway that led up to the next level. Minutes later, he was in another tunnel exactly similar to the first one, walking southward again.

But now he was more careful. He watched the ground carefully, making sure that he didn't step on anything that would snap or rattle. The Nipe was still quite a distance away-three-quarters of a mile, or so-but taking the chance that the beast couldn't hear him might be deadly dangerous. The robot rat that he was following led him along a path that had been unobtrusively cleared of rubble by the robot rats over a period of months, but the robots weren't the only rats in the place. He kept his eyes on the path.

A while later, the voice in his ear said: "A hundred yards to go, Barbell."

"I know," Stanton whispered. "He hasn't moved?"

"No. I'll yell if he does. You don't need to talk any more. His ears might pick up even that whisper."

He hasn't moved, Stanton thought. *Not for all this time. Not since I came down into his private domain. All this time, he has been sitting motionless-waiting. Wouldn't it be funny if he were dead? If his heart had stopped, or something. Wouldn't that be absolutely hilarious? Wouldn't that be a big joke on everybody? Especially me.*

Ahead was the large area that had been one of the major junction points of the tunnel network. This was the area that the Nipe had taken over to build his home-away-from-home. Here were his workshops, his laboratories, his storerooms.

And somewhere here was the Nipe.

He came out of the tunnel into another passenger-loading area. Just to his left was another short stairway that led up to a slightly higher level. He moved slowly and quietly. He didn't want to fight down here on the tracks, and he didn't want to be caught just yet.

Cautiously he lifted himself to the platform where long-gone passengers had once waited for long-gone trains.

The quality of the illumination at the head of the stairs was different from that which he had been used to for the past three hours. He lifted off the infra-red goggles. Enough light spilled over from the Nipe's lair to give him illumination to see by. Silently, he put the goggles on the floor of the platform. He wouldn't need them again.

Then, step by step, he walked up the concrete stairway.

At the head of the stairs, he paused to get his bearings.

The illumination was not bright, but it was enough to —

"Barbell! He's heard you! Watch it!"

But Stanton had already heard the movement of the Nipe. He jerked off the communicator and threw it down the stairs behind him. He wanted no encumbrances now!

He ran quickly out into the center of the big underground room, away from the open stairwell.

And then, as fast as any express train that had ever moved through these subterranean ways, the Nipe came around a corner thirty feet away, his four violet eyes gleaming, his limbs rippling beneath his centipede-like body.

From fifteen feet away, he launched himself through the air, his outstretched hands ready to kill.

But Stanton's marvelous neuromuscular system was already in action.

At this stage of the game, it would be utter suicide to let the Nipe get in close. Stanton couldn't fend off eight grasping hands with his own two. He leaped to one side, and the Nipe got his first surprise in ten years when Stanton's fist slammed against the side of his snouted head, knocking him in the direction opposite that in which Stanton had moved.

The Nipe landed, turned, and charged back toward the man. This time he reared up, using his two rearmost pairs of limbs for locomotion, while the two forward pairs were held out, ready to kill.

He got surprise number two when Stanton's fist landed on the tip of his rather sensitive snout, rocking his head back. His own hands met nothing but air, and by the time he had recovered from the blow, Stanton was well back, out of the way.

He's so small! Stanton thought wonderingly. Even when he reared up, the Nipe's head was only three feet above the concrete floor.

The Nipe came in again-more cautiously this time.

Stanton punched again with a straight right. The Nipe moved his head aside, and Stanton's knuckles merely grazed the side of the alien's head, just below the lower right eye.

At the same time, one of the Nipe's hands swung in in a chopping right hook that took Stanton just below the ribs. Stanton leaped back with a gasp of pain.

The Nipe didn't use fists. He used his open hand, fingers together, like a judo fighter.

The Nipe came forward, and, as Stanton danced back, the Nipe made a grab for his ankle, almost catching it. There were too many hands to watch!

Stanton had two advantages: weight and reach. His arms were almost half again as long as the Nipe's.

Against that, the Nipe had all those hands; and with his low center of gravity and four-footed stance, it would be hard to knock him down. On the other hand, if Stanton lost his footing, the fight would be over fast.

Stanton lunged suddenly forward and planted a left in the Nipe's right upper eye, then followed it with a right uppercut to the Nipe's jaw as his head snapped back. The Nipe's four hands cut inward from the sides like sword blades, but they found no target.

Backing away, Stanton realized he had another advantage. The Nipe couldn't throw a straight jab! His shoulders-if that's what they should be called-were narrow and the upper arm bones weren't articulated properly for such a blow. The alien could throw a mean hook, but he had to get in close to deliver it.

On the other side of the coin was the fact that the Nipe knew plenty about human anatomy-from the bones out. Stanton's knowledge of Nipe anatomy was almost totally superficial.

He wished he knew if and where the Nipe had a solar plexus. He would like to punch something soft for a change.

Instead, he tried for another eye. He danced in, jabbed, and danced out. The Nipe had ducked again, taking the blow on the side of his head.

Then the Nipe came in low, at an angle, trying for the groin. For his troubles, he got a knee in the jaw that staggered him badly. One grasping hand clutched at Stanton's right thigh and grabbed hard. Stanton swung his fist down like a pendulum and knocked the arm aside.

But there was a slight limp in his movements as he back-pedaled away from the Nipe. That full-handed pinch had hurt like the very devil!

Stanton was angry now, with the hot, controlled anger of a fighting man. He stepped in quickly and slammed two fast hard jabs into the point of the Nipe's snout, jarring the monster backward. And this time it was the Nipe who scuttled back out of the way.

Stanton moved in fast to press his advantage and landed a beaut on the Nipe's lower left eye. Then he tried a body blow. It wasn't too successful. The alien had an endoskeleton, but he also had a tough hide that was somewhat like thick, leathery chitin.

Stanton pulled back, getting out of the way of the Nipe's open-handed judo cuts.

His fists were beginning to hurt, and his leg was paining him badly where the Nipe had clamped onto it. And his ribs were throbbing where the Nipe had landed that single blow.

And then he realized that, so far, the Nipe had only landed that one blow!

One punch and one pinch, Stanton thought with a touch of awe. *The only other damage he's inflicted has been to my knuckles!*

The Nipe charged in again, then he leaped suddenly and clawed for Stanton's face with his first pair of hands. The second and third pairs chopped in toward the man's body. The last pair propelled him off the floor.

Stanton stepped back and drove in a long, hard right, hitting him just below the jaw, where his throat would have been if he had been human.

The Nipe arced backward in a half somersault and landed flat on his back.

Stanton backed up a little more, waiting, while the Nipe wiggled feebly for a moment. *The Marquis of Queensberry should have lived to see this*, he thought.

The Nipe rolled over and crouched on all eight limbs. His violet eyes watched Stanton, but the man could read no expression on that inhuman face.

"You did not kill."

For a moment, Stanton found it hard to believe that the hissing, guttural voice had come from the crouching monster.

"You did not even try *to kill."*

"I have no wish to kill you," Stanton said evenly.

"I can see that. Do you ... Are you..." He stopped, as if baffled. *"There are not the proper words. Do you follow the Customs?"*

Stanton felt a surge of triumph. This was what George Yoritomo had guessed might happen!

"If I must kill you," Stanton said carefully, "I, myself, will do the honors. You will not go uneaten."

The Nipe sagged a little, relaxing all over. *"I had hoped it was so. It was the only thinkable thing. I saw you on the television, and it was only thinkable that you came for me."*

Stanton sighed inwardly. That part of Colonel Mannheim's strategy had worked, too. The Nipe had seen all the publicity releases that had been so carefully tailored for him.

"I knew you were out on the asteroids," the Nipe went on. *"But I had decided that you had come to kill. Since you did not, what are your thoughts, Stanley Martin?"*

"That we should help each other," Stanton said.

It was as simple as that.

Stanton sat in his hotel room, smoking a cigarette, staring at the wall, and thinking.

He was alone again. All the fuss and feathers and foofaraw were over. Dr. Farnsworth was in another room of the suite, making his plans for a complete physical examination of the Nipe. Dr. George Yoritomo was having the time of his life, holding a conversation with the Nipe, drawing the alien out, and getting him to talk about his own race and their history.

And Stanley Martin was plotting the next phase of the capture-the cover-up.

Stanton smiled a little. Colonel Mannheim had been a great one for planning, all right. Every little detail was taken care of. It had sometimes made his plans more complex than necessary, Stanton suspected. Mannheim had tended to try to account for every possible eventuality, and, after he had done that, he had set aside a few reserves here and there, just in case they might be useful if something unforeseen happened.

All things considered, the Government had certainly done the right thing. And, in picking Mannheim, they had picked the right man.

Stanton got up, walked over to the window, and looked down at the streets of Government City, eight floors below.

What would those people down there think if they were told the true story of the Nipe? What would the average citizen say if he discovered that, at this very moment, the Nipe was being treated almost as an honored guest of the Government? More, what would he say if he suspected that the Nipe-the horrible, murderous, man-eating Nipe-could have been killed easily at any time during the past six years?

Would it be possible for anyone to explain to the common average man that, in the long run, the knowledge possessed by the Nipe was tremendously more valuable to the race of Man than the lives of a few individuals?

Could those people down there, and the others like them all over the world, be made to understand that, by his own lights, the Nipe had been behaving in the most civilized and gentlemanly fashion he knew? Could they ever be made to understand that, because of the tremendous wealth of priceless information stored in that alien brain, the Nipe's life had to be preserved at any cost?

Or would they scream for blood?

Dr. Farnsworth assumed that Stanley Martin was going to spread a story about the Nipe's death —a carefully concocted story about how Stanley Martin had found the beast and the police had killed it. There might, Farnsworth assumed, be a carefully made "corpse" for the mob to hiss at. Maybe Farnsworth was right. But Stanton had the feeling that Martin and George Yoritomo had something else up their collective sleeve.

The phone hummed. Stanton walked over, thumbed the answer button, and watched George Yoritomo's face take shape on the screen.

"Bart! I have just had the privilege of viewing the tapes of your fight with our friend, the Nipe. Incredible! I watched the original on the screen, of course, but I had to run the tapes. I wanted to slow it down, so that I could see what actually happened. Magnificent, that right of yours! *So!*" He jabbed a fist out, shadowboxing with Stanton over the phone circuit.

"Awww, it weren't nuthin', Maw," Stanton drawled. "I jes' sorta flang out a fist an' he got in the way."

"Of course! But such a fling! Seriously, Bart, I want to run those tapes over again, and I want you to tell me, as best you can, just what went on in your mind at each stage of the fight. It will be most informative."

"You mean right now? I have an appointment —"

Yoritomo waved a hand. "No, no. Later. Take your time. But I am honestly amazed that you won so easily. I knew you were good, and I was certain you'd win, but I must admit that I honestly expected you to be injured."

Stanton looked down at his bandaged hands and felt the ache of his broken rib and the pain of the blue bruise on his thigh. In spite of the way it looked, he had actually been hurt worse than the Nipe had. That boy was *tough*!

"The trouble was that he couldn't adapt himself to fighting in a new way, just as you predicted," he told Yoritomo. "He fought me, I assume, in just the way he would have fought another Nipe. And that didn't work. I had the reach on him, and I could maneuver faster. Besides, he can't throw a straight punch with those shoulders of his."

"It appeared to me," Yoritomo said with a broad grin, "that you were fighting him as you would fight another human being. Eh?"

Stanton grinned back. "I was, in a modified way. But I wasn't confined to a pattern. Besides, I won-the Nipe didn't. And that's all that counts."

"It is, indeed. Well, I'll let you know when I'm ready for your impressions of the fight. Probably tomorrow some time-say, in the afternoon?"

"Fine."

George Yoritomo nodded his thanks, and his image collapsed and faded from the screen.

Stanton walked back over to the window, but this time he looked at the horizon, not the street.

George Yoritomo had called him "Bart". It's funny, Stanton thought, how habit can get the best of a man. Yoritomo had known the truth all along. And now he knew that his pupil-or patient-whichever it was-was aware of the truth. And still, he had called him "Bart".

And I still think of myself as Bart, he thought. *I probably always will.*

And why not? Why shouldn't he? Martin Stanton no longer existed-in a sense, he had never existed. And in actual fact, he had never had much of a real existence. He was only a bad dream. He had always been a bad dream. And now that the dream was over, only "Bart" was real.

He thought back, remembering George Yoritomo's explanation.

"Take two people," he had said. "Two people genetically identical. Damage one of them so badly that he is helpless and useless-to himself and to others. Damage him so badly that he is always only a step away from death.

"The vague telepathic bond that always links identical twins (they 'think alike', they say) becomes unbalanced under such conditions.

"Normally, there is a give-and-take. One mind is as strong as the other, and each preserves the sense of his own identity, since the two different sets of sense receptors give different viewpoints. But if one of the twins is damaged badly enough, then something must happen to that telepathic linkage.

"Usually it is broken.

"But the link between you and your brother was not broken. Instead, it became a one-way channel.

"What happens in such a case? The damaged brother, in order to escape the intolerable prison of his own body, becomes a receptor for the stronger brother's thoughts. The weaker feels as the stronger feels. The experience of the one becomes the experience of the other-the thrill of running after a baseball, the pride of doing something clever with the hands, the touch of a girl's kiss upon the lips-all these become the property of the weaker, since he is receiving the thoughts of the stronger. There is, of course, no flow in the other direction. The stronger brother has no way of knowing that his every thought is being duplicated in his brother's mind.

"In effect, the damaged brother ceases to think. The thoughts in his mind are those of the healthy brother. The feeling of identity becomes almost complete.

"To the outside observer, the damaged brother appears to be a cataleptic schizophrenic, completely cut off from reality. And, in a sense, he is."

Stanton walked over to the nightstand by the bed, took another cigarette from the pack, lit it, and looked at the smoke curling up from the tip.

So Martin became a cataleptic schizophrenic, he thought.

The mind of Martin had ceased to think at all. The "Bart" part of him had not wanted to be disturbed by the garbled, feeble sensory impressions that "Mart's" body provided. Like many another schizophrenic, Martin had been living in a little world cut off from the actual physical world around his body.

The difference between Martin's condition and that of the ordinary schizophrenic had been that Martin's little dream world had actually existed. It had been an almost exact counterpart of the world that had existed in the perfectly sane, rational mind of his brother, Bart. It had grown and developed as Bart had, fed by the one-way telepathic flow from the stronger mind to the weaker.

There had been two Barts-and no Mart at all.

But there had been only one human being between them. Bart Stanton had been a strong, capable, intelligent, active human being. The duplicate of his mind was just a recording in the mind of a useless, radiation-blasted hulk.

And then the Neurophysical Institute had come into the picture. A new process had been developed by Dr. Farnsworth and his crew, by which a human being could be reconstructed-made, literally, into a superman. All the techniques had been worked out in careful and minute detail. But there was one major drawback. Any normal human body would resist the process-to the death, if necessary-just as a normal human body will resist a skin graft from an alien donor or the injection of an alien protein.

But the radiation-damaged body of Martin Stanton had had no resistance of that kind. It had long been known that deep-penetrating ionizing radiation had that effect on an organism. The ability to resist was weakened, almost destroyed.

With Martin Stanton's body-perhaps-the process might work.

So Bartholomew Stanton, who had become Martin's legal guardian after the death of their mother, had given permission for the series of operations that would rebuild his crippled brother.

The telepathic link, of course, had to be shut off-for a time, at least. If it remained intact, Martin would never be able to think for himself, no matter what was done to his body. Part of that cutting-off process could be done during the treatment of Martin-but only if Bartholomew would co-operate. He had done his part. He had submitted to deep hypnosis, and had allowed himself to be convinced that his name was Stanley Martin, to think of himself as Stanley Martin. The Martin name was one that the real Martin's mind would reject utterly. That mind wanted nothing to do with anything named Martin.

"Stanley Martin," then, had gone out to the asteroids. In his mind had been implanted the further instructions that he was not to return to Earth nor to attempt to investigate the Nipe under any circumstances. The simple change of name and environment had been just enough to snap the link during a time when Martin's brain had been inactivated by cold therapy and anesthetics.

Only the sense of identity had remained. The patient was still "Bart"—but now he was being forced to think for himself.

Mannheim had used them both, naturally. Colonel Mannheim had the ability to use anyone at hand, including himself, to get a job done.

Stanton looked at his watch. It was almost time.

Mannheim had sent for "Stanley Martin" when the time had come for him to return in order to give the Nipe data that he would be sure to misinterpret. A special series of code phrases in the message had released "Stanley Martin" from the hypnotic suggestions that had held him for so long. He knew now that he was Bartholomew Stanton.

And so do I, thought the man by the window. *We have a lot to straighten out, we two.*

There was a knock at the door.

Stanton walked over and opened it, trying not to think.

It was like looking into a mirror.

"Hello, Bart," he said.

"Hello, Bart," said the other.

In that instant, complete telepathic linkage was restored. In that instant, they both knew what only one of them had known before-that, for a time, the telepathic flow had been one-way again, but this time in the opposite direction-that "Stanley Martin" had been shaken that afternoon when his own mind had become the receptor for the other's thoughts, and he had experienced completely the entire battle with the Nipe. His release from the posthypnotic suggestion had made it possible.

There was no need for further words.

E duobus unum.

There was unity without loss of identity.

www.ingramcontent.com/pod-product-compliance
Lightning Source LLC
Chambersburg PA
CBHW071335130626
46556CB00004B/1919